'Our new Book of the Week is ... a great new voice and definite Pri...

'I laughed and squirmed my way through *The Real Rebecca*, the sparkling and spookily accurate diary of a Dublin teenager. It's stonkingly good and I haven't laughed so much since reading Louise Rennison. Teenage girls ... will love Rebecca to bits!'

'This book is fantastic! Rebecca is sweet, funny and down-to-earth, and I adored her friends, her quirky parents, her changeable but ultimately loving older sister and the swoonworthy Paperboy.'

'What is it like inside the mind of a teenage girl? It's a strange, confused and frustrated place, as Anna Carey's first novel *The Real Rebecca* makes clear ... A laugh-out-loud story of a fourteen-year-old girl, Rebecca Rafferty.'

'The story rattles along at a glorious rate – with plenty of witty asides. Rebecca herself is a thoroughly likeable heroine – angsty and mixed-up but warm-hearted and feisty.'

'Carey's teen voice is spot-on.'

PRAISE FOR REBECCA'S RULES

'A gorgeous book! ... So funny, sweet, bright. I loved it.'

Marian Keyes

'Amusing from the first page ... better than Adrian Mole! Highly recommended.'

lovereading4kids.co.uk

'The teen voice is spot on ... Carey captures the excitement, camaraderie and tensions brilliantly.'

Books for Keeps

'John Kowalski is an inspired creation.'

Irish Independent

'Sure to be a favourite with fans of authors such as Sarah Webb and Judi Curtin.'

Children's Books Ireland's Recommended Reads 2012

PRAISE FOR REBECCA ROCKS

'A charming, uplifting story.'

Irish Independent

'Carey hits the mark in terms of finding an authentic teenage voice.'

Inismagazine.ie

'The pages in Carey's novel in which her young lesbian character announces her coming out to her friends and in which they give their reactions are superbly written: tone is everything, and it could not be better handled than it is here.'

Irish Times

'A bright and breezy read.'

The Sunday Business Post

'A hilarious new book, perfect for the summer. Cleverly written, witty and smart.'

writing.ie

'Rebecca Rafferty ... is something of a *Books for Keeps* favourite ... Honest, real, touching, a terrific piece of writing.'

Books for Keeps

Anna Carey is a freelance journalist from Drumcondra in Dublin who has written for the *Irish Times*, *Irish Independent* and many other publications. Anna joined her first band when she was fifteen and went on to sing and play with several bands over the next fifteen years. Her last band, El Diablo, released two albums and toured all over the country. Anna's first book, *The Real Rebecca*, was published in 2011, and, to her great surprise, it went on to win the Senior Children's Book prize at the Irish Book Awards. To the delight of many readers, Rebecca returned in the critically acclaimed *Rebecca's Rules* and *Rebecca Rocks*.

REBECCA

is always

RIGHT

Anna Carey

IRISH BOOK AWARD WINNER

THE O'BRIEN PRESS
DUBLIN

First published 2014 by The O'Brien Press Ltd,
12 Terenure Road East, Rathgar, Dublin 6, Ireland.
Tel: +353 1 4923333; Fax: +353 1 4922777
E-mail: books@obrien.ie
Website: www.obrien.ie

ISBN: 978-1-84717-565-6

10 9 8 7 6 5 4 3 2 1
19 18 17 16 15 14

Layout and design: The O'Brien Press Ltd.
Cover illustrations: Chris Judge
Printed and bound by CPI Group (UK) Ltd, Croydon, CR0 4YY
The paper in this book is produced using pulp from
managed forests.

The O'Brien Press receives financial assistance from

ACKNOWLEDGEMENTS

Thanks to Clare Kelly, Susan Houlden, my ever-patient editor, and everyone at The O'Brien Press; Helen Carr for all her support and encouragement; Chris Judge for being the best cover artist I could ever have hoped for (and for putting an excellent pug on the cover of this book); the extended Freyne and Carey families; my husband, Patrick Freyne, who kept me going through what was an unusually stressful writing process (including the death of our cranky, yet much-loved, cat Ju Ju); and most of all to everyone who has read and enjoyed the first three Rebecca books. This one wouldn't exist without you.

To my nephews Arlo, Eli and Stanley, in the hope that you will make each other laugh as much as your mothers and aunts did (though maybe you could fight a bit more quietly than we did, just for your parents' sake)

SATURDAY ☺

There are only forty-eight hours left before I go back to school, and I'm going to have to spend at least two of them with a baby who hates me. Well, I think it hates me. Every time I go anywhere near it, it turns bright red and starts roaring, and then it gets sick. Usually on me. It belongs to my lovely godmother, Daisy, and how such a nice, cheerful woman and her nice, cheerful husband managed to produce such an angry baby is a mystery to me. Mum says I'm being ridiculous and there's no way a six-month-old baby could hate anyone, but I'm pretty sure it can.

'It's a small baby!' said Mum. 'They all spend a lot of their time turning red and roaring. It's just what they do. It's nothing personal!'

'Well, it doesn't seem to do it when you pick it up,' I said, and Mum couldn't really argue with that because it's true. So in typical style, she just ignored my clever comeback.

'Whether it – I mean she – hates you or not, you're still coming to Daisy's this afternoon,' she said.

So that's that. I will have to spend two (or more, depending on the traffic) of my precious final hours of freedom being sicked on and roared at. It's so unfair. And what makes it even worse is the fact that Rachel isn't coming because it's Tom-the-Perfect-Boyfriend's birthday, so she's going to some ridiculous birthday dinner in his house with all his family and then into town with a gang of their friends.

I told Mum that Rachel would be back from Daisy's house in plenty of time to go to Saint Tom's big party so there was no real reason why she couldn't go, but Rachel insisted that she had to 'get Tom's present ready'. Which was, as I pointed out, a terrible excuse because we all know what her present for him is; it's a cool t-shirt she bought on the internet and a book he's wanted to read for ages. How long can that take to 'get ready'? All she has to do is wrap it! And that'll only take about two minutes. It's not as if it's some giant weirdly shaped thing like a bike or a drum kit. But Rachel never has to do anything she doesn't want to do. Unlike me.

Oh, I can't believe we have to go back to school on Monday. Well, I can believe it, but I don't like it. It's not only that the weather's been gorgeous (unlike last year), which makes the thought of having to sit indoors all day wearing that hideous uniform even more awful, but this summer has been so much fun. We've done so many cool things that going back to boring old geography and German and homework seems even worse.

We were all discussing this yesterday when I met up with Cass, Alice and Liz in town.

'I don't want summer to be over!' said Cass. 'This summer was way better than last year.'

'It really was,' I said. 'Lots more happened for a start. I mean, first of all I got my hair cut into a fringe. I know that turned out to be a mistake, but it was quite a dramatic way to start off the holidays.'

'It was a bold move,' said Liz. 'I wish I'd got to see it in its full glory.'

'It did look really good for a day or so before it went all weird and fluffy,' said Cass. 'It really suited her.'

'And then you told me you were gay,' I said to Cass. 'Actually, I should probably have put that before the fringe thing – it's a bit more important.'

'Just a bit,' said Cass.

'And then we went on the summer rock camp and learned loads of useful stuff about being in a band,' said Alice. 'It was quite a practical summer when you think about it. And we wrote lots of new songs for Hey Dollface.'

This is all true. We have definitely expanded our band's repertoire. And we made lots of cool new friends there too. So that was all good.

'Of course, we did have to put up with Charlie and his gang,' said Cass.

I shuddered as I remembered those awful, obnoxious boys.

'But people stood up to them in the end,' said Alice.

'And even Karen turned out to have a good side,' I said. 'Which was a very pleasant surprise considering she's basically our enemy.'

'Well, that was sort of pleasant,' said Cass. 'I mean, obviously it was a good thing that she did something decent, and I do really appreciate it, but it did make me feel a bit weird. We're just used to her being annoying, so it was hard to know what to do when she actually did something really nice.'

'This is true,' I said. 'I wonder will she still be as annoying when we go back on Monday? Or will she have had a complete change of heart and decide that she loves us all?'

'I don't think that's very likely,' said Alice.

I'm pretty sure she's right. But anyway, the whole camp was generally brilliant, and I wish it could have lasted all summer.

'You know, I thought nothing good would ever happen again after the camp ended,' I said, stretching back in my seat. 'Everything felt really flat. It was like when the school musical ended, only even worse because we just did the musical for a few evenings a week, and the summer camp was all day, every day, so it was basically our entire life for a whole month. But actually the last month of the holidays has been pretty good.'

And it really has. We've stayed in touch with our camp friends online and have met up with them a few times (well, most of them – no one has seen the mysterious Small Paula since the camp ended). And even though I was sort of worried that I would be abandoned to my lonely single devices now both Cass and Alice were going out with people, that didn't happen.

'Much as I want to see Richard,' said Alice, a few days after the summer camp ended, 'I need to see you two as well. I can't survive on Richard alone.' Then she looked worried. 'That doesn't sound like I'm being mean about either you or him, does it?'

I assured her it didn't. It makes sense. Even in the brief time when I was properly going out with Paperboy, I still wanted to hang out with Cass and Alice too.

Of course, there were still a few times this summer when I'd have liked to have done stuff with them, but they were off with their beloveds doing … well, whatever people do when they're going out with someone. It's been so long since I was going out with anyone that I've forgotten what it's like. Actually, the last person I went out with was John Kowalski, and

I spent most of that time listening to him go on about what a genius he was. I don't think most relationships are like that (at least I hope not. I can't imagine Liz or Richard boasting about how great they are for hours on end. Or Cass or Alice, for that matter).

But anyway, on the days when Cass and Alice were off on their own with Liz and Richard, I just read or wrote stuff or hung out with Jane and some of the other people from the camp. There were only a couple of days when I felt like I didn't really have anything to do or anyone to do it with, but when I mentioned to my mum that I was bored, she just laughed and reminded me that this used to happen last year, before Cass or Alice were going out with anyone, so I suppose being a little bit bored sometimes is just part of summer. And at least I get on really well with Liz and Richard and we can hang out together. Imagine if Cass and Alice were going out with people I didn't actually like.

Oh God, Mum is calling me to come and visit my baby enemy now. I'd rather have nothing to do than be roared at for hours on end.

LATER

The baby still hates me. Not only did it get sick on me, it actually headbutted me! I hope my nose isn't broken. It feels okay now, but you never know. Even Mum had to admit the headbutting was quite dramatic, though she claimed that the baby didn't really mean to headbutt me, and that I just leaned over it when it was lifting its head up and it butted me by accident. But I think it knew exactly what it was doing. Mum is sure that my nose isn't broken, but I just hope I don't develop some terrible nose problems because if I do it will all be that baby's fault.

It was nice to see Daisy, though. She gave me a book called *I Capture the Castle*, which she says she read when she was my age and which she thinks I will like. I need something entertaining to distract me from the horror of going back to school in just a few hours (well, about thirty-five hours now. But I'm going to spend at least fourteen of them sleeping, so it's not that many really).

By the way, as I thought, Rachel was just lazing around on the couch when we got back. So much for her 'ooh, I have loads of things to do for Tom!' nonsense. And I just know it only took her a few minutes to wrap his present. She did use very nice wrapping paper and a lovely ribbon, but, to be honest, that's the least she could do because when it was her birthday he got her a bottle of fancy Chanel perfume that smells gorgeous. It must have cost a fortune; it looked so posh in its little box. Anyway, I can't believe she got out of a visit to the dreadful baby just for wrapping a t-shirt and a book, even if the paper was fancy and she wrapped it all up with a posh checked ribbon. She gets away with murder.

SUNDAY ☼

Last day of the holidays! I met up with Cass and Alice in town to toast the best summer ever and to drown our sorrows (in hot chocolate for me and Cass and peppermint tea for Alice) about going back to school.

'The very worst thing about going into third year,' said Cass, 'is that you just know all the teachers are going to spend the entire year reminding us it's our Junior Cert year. As if we didn't know already.'

'Well, we are going to have to put our heads down a bit this year,' said Alice, looking a bit worried.

'But we all know this,' Cass pointed out. 'So Mrs Harrington reminding us about it every five minutes, in every English class, is hardly going to help.'

Ugh, it certainly won't.

'Sometimes it feels as if we've got nothing to look forward to but exams and exams and more exams for years and years,' I said.

'I know,' said Cass. 'I mean, we've got the Junior Cert, and then maybe transition year won't have exams, but after that we'll have fifth-year summer tests, and then the Leaving, and then we'll hopefully have college for three or four years, depending on what we do and where we go. That's six more years of exams at the very least!'

'And then what if you did a Master's?' said Alice. 'That'd be more exams, wouldn't it?'

'My dad did a PhD,' I said. 'He didn't finish college until he was, like, twenty-five.'

We all looked at each other gloomily. Actually, now I think about it, technically Dad never left college because after he got his PhD he stayed there forever working as a lecturer. And I don't think you actually have to do exams if you do a PhD. But still, you have to keep doing school-ish sort of work for years on end, which doesn't sound like fun to me.

Anyway, then Alice suggested ordering a slice of cake and

sharing it between us, so we did, and that made us cheer up a bit. We couldn't afford to get a slice each after our beverages – hot chocolate is surprisingly expensive. I wish I actually liked coffee, or even tea. It seems a bit babyish only getting hot chocolates when we go to cafés. Coffee is so much more grown up, and I actually do like the smell of it. But I've tried drinking it a good few times and I just don't like it.

But you never know, I might still grow into it. Mum once told me that she didn't even like tea until she was in college, and now she drinks about seven cups of it a day. And Daisy said she didn't like coffee until she was about twenty-two and now she can't function without it. Although now I think about it, maybe being totally addicted to a hot drink isn't such a good thing either.

Still, surely anything that could make me feel a bit more awake when I get up in the middle of the night tomorrow (okay, a quarter to eight in the morning, but it's early in comparison to the last month) to go to school would be a plus. Oh, I wish we didn't have to go back now! Especially as we bumped into a couple of our summer-camp friends today on our way to our various bus stops, which reminded me again of how cool the camp was. We were just walking past the Central Bank when we met Tall Paula, the cool, gothy girl from Beaumont who was in the band Exquisite Corpse, and none other than Small Paula, the enigmatic solo artist.

Apparently they'd bumped into each other looking at guitar pedals in a music shop and were walking back towards their bus stops together. It was very nice to see them. Small Paula didn't say very much, but then she never did, and she looked quite pleased to see us (well, as much of her as we could see beneath her giant fringe). Neither of them are looking forward to going back to school either. Tall Paula said her parents have said that as well as one band practice a week, she can only go out with her friends after school or at the weekend once a month all year because of the Junior Cert.

'They're going to write down all my outings on the kitchen calendar to make sure I don't go over the limit by accident,' she said miserably.

This seems pretty harsh to me. I mean, I know we were getting stressed at the thought of our never-ending exams, but I don't think it's physically possible to work every single day even if you wanted to (which I certainly don't). But everyone's parents are acting as if we were doing our Leaving Cert, which is a bit ridiculous.

Tall Paula did remind us of something cool, though – the band practice space that's going to be opening in the Knitting

Factory. Veronica, who ran the band part of the summer camp, has arranged for the studios to offer teenage bands from the camp access to the spaces for a small fee, and the camp mentors are going to have regular classes and stuff too. We hadn't heard from them yet, but the Paulas met Veronica today when they were coming out of the music shop.

'Veronica said they're just finalising details now,' said Tall Paula. 'And she said they'll definitely contact all of us once it's sorted, so in a few weeks we'll all have somewhere to practise in town! Maybe I could tell my mum it's a special extra Junior Cert music class or something.'

But the studio space isn't all. We should be able to put on gigs too, which is cool, because it is very hard to find somewhere to play a gig if you are under eighteen. This is because people who run venues are more concerned with making loads of money from selling BOOZE than encouraging the musicians of the future. Ages ago, Liz thought she'd found a venue that would let us play all-ages afternoon gigs, but it didn't work out because of insurance or something boring like that.

Anyway, if Veronica's thing works out, and Tall Paula said she seemed pretty sure it would, we will be able to play gigs regularly! And hopefully we'll get to see lots of the camp people regularly again too, because they'll be doing stuff at the Knitting Factory too.

'There's a whole arts space thing at the back of the Knitting Factory,' said Tall Paula. 'So they're talking about working with the mentors from the other bits of the camp and having art and drama workshops and other stuff too.'

That would all be so, so cool. It would be like a continuation of the summer camp. I just hope our parents let us all out of the house long enough to actually go there. I have a horrible feeling mine won't. My dad just stuck his head around the corner of my room and said he hoped I wasn't going to stay up late writing, because I have school tomorrow. It's only half past nine! Are they actually going to make me go to bed at this time every night all year?! Surely not. Humans only need about eight hours' sleep and I'm hardly going to get up at half five in the morning.

Ugh. This time tomorrow I might actually be doing homework. What a thought.

MONDAY ☺

I am not doing any homework, but that's mostly because I am so, so tired. I had forgotten how exhausting stupid school is. It doesn't really make sense because when we were at the summer camp we were standing up and moving around and DOING STUFF all day and I always felt fine in the evenings. But after one day of just sitting at a bunch of stupid desks, I'm so tired I can barely stand. It's so unfair.

Today wasn't totally and utterly bad, of course. It was nice to see some of the people we didn't see as much of over the summer, like Emma and Jessie. And even though we have Mrs Harrington for English again this year, the class was actually quite interesting because we've been reading some good books for English and, to my great surprise, Mrs Harrington wasn't as annoying as she usually is. In fact, she didn't make a single reference to my mother's books, which is not like her at all as she is scarily obsessed with Mum's boring stories about kindly old ladies. As she hadn't seen me for months, I'd assumed she'd be dying to ask me questions about 'what lovely tales your mammy is thinking of now' (that is how she always talks, so you can see how annoying she is). But no. In fact, she was so quiet I'd actually be worried that there was something seriously wrong with her if she hadn't seemed pretty cheerful too. She just seemed a bit distracted. I suppose I should just be thankful and not question it too much.

Actually, I always feel a bit bad giving out about Mrs Harrington now, who is irritating but means well. I do not, however, feel bad about giving out about Vanessa Finn, who does not mean well at all and who has somehow become even more annoying since the last time I saw her, which was only a month ago at the summer camp. Apparently a few weeks ago she auditioned for a big part in an advertising campaign, and she's totally convinced that she's going to get it.

'I'm expecting a call at any moment,' she said at lunch, making sure everyone in the room could hear her.

'I'm sure they'll ring soon,' said Caroline, Vanessa's best friend.

'It's so exciting, Vanessa!' said Karen Rodgers, and I had to remind myself of how Karen had stood up for Cass at the summer camp because otherwise her smarmy tone would have made me get sick. 'And you totally deserve it! An actor with your skills deserves a bigger audience.'

Also, it turns out that getting this ad could be Vanessa's only chance of being on television this year because her appearance in the reality show *My Big Birthday Bash* has been cancelled! Or rather, the entire show has been cancelled. I am quite relieved because we were all at her birthday party when they filmed it back in February and I don't particularly want to see myself on telly. And Vanessa is pleased about it too.

'Yeah, reality TV wasn't the right outlet for my talents,' she said.

Though of course we all know she didn't want the show to air because her party ended up with her being knocked into a cake by a pink pony. But no one mentioned that. Cass caught my eye and made a little neighing sound, but that was all.

I did notice that Karen's sidekick, Alison, was looking a bit bored when Vanessa was going on about all this. Ever since Karen and Vanessa became friendly I have been hoping Caroline and Alison would team up and escape their clutches, because both of them are quite nice when they're not being sidekicks. But it doesn't seem to have happened yet. Though Alison was on some sort of computer course during the summer and she was talking about that to Emma after maths (oh maths, I have not missed you) this afternoon. So maybe she's escaping very, very slowly.

Another person who hasn't changed much is Miss Kelly. She marched into our first geography class of the year and immediately started going on about her environmentally friendly summer holiday. She cycled all over France with some of her friends. It's quite impressive, especially for someone of her age.

'If I could have kayaked to France, that's what I'd have done,' she said proudly. 'Unfortunately, I had to use a bigger boat.'

'Like a rowing boat?' asked Jessie, impressed.

'Sadly no,' said Miss Kelly. 'The ferry. But after that, it was pedals all the way. Soon we were cycling along the roads of Brittany, stopping only for the odd baguette and slice of local cheese.' And on and on she went for about five years. Actually, she did stop, after a while, so she could tell us about the horrors of fracking, which seems to be a way of getting natural gas from under the ground by destroying everything on top of the ground. It was quite scary, but I must admit it was more interesting than hearing yet another story of how she and her mates managed to cycle up a French mountain. You'd think they were elite athletes doing the Tour de France, rather than a bunch of middle-aged teachers cycling around the country-side, eating loads of Brie.

Oh, I'm actually too tired to write any more. I'm going to go down and watch telly for a while instead. Luckily the only homework we got was to read something in the history book, and I've already done that. Surely my parents can't expect me to do extra study after just one day of school? It's bad enough that they change the wifi password practically every day to make sure I'm not messing around on the internet on my phone.

TUESDAY ☾

I was actually driven out of our classroom at lunchtime today by Vanessa going on about that stupid ad campaign. She still doesn't know whether she's got the part or not, but when we were all sitting around the classroom eating our sandwiches Jessie foolishly asked her what the ad was actually for, and that set her off.

'It's for Bluebird Bakery,' said Vanessa in a very important way, and we all tried to look as if we weren't impressed or even as though we didn't know what Bluebird Bakery is. But I was impressed, a bit, even though I'd have died rather than admit it to Vanessa. Bluebird Bakery is a really big brand and they always have big posters everywhere as well as regular ads on the TV. And they do make very nice biscuits. Of course, they usually have quite cool telly ads too, so surely they won't let Vanessa appear in them. I mean, the sight of her messing around with some biscuits would certainly put me off eating them.

But the school musical did teach me I should never underestimate Vanessa – before the auditions I was convinced she'd be rubbish and then she turned out to be really brilliant, much as I hated to admit it. So maybe she actually would be good at making people want to eat biscuits. Anyway, she seems totally sure that she's going to get this job and I couldn't bear listening to her anymore so I went to the library to see if they'd got in any new books this term. Luckily they have, including a few that look really good – there's one called *Code Name Verity* about girls working undercover in France during the second world war which looks brilliant.

In fact, there were so many interesting-looking new books I wanted to get out about five of them, but we're only allowed take out three at a time. A few sixth years always run the library at lunchtime when the librarian is on her break, and it turns out that Rachel's friend Jenny is one of them this year. I was hoping she might let me take out extra books (after all, I am her best friend's sister, and she's usually quite nice to me – she came to our very first gig at the Battle of the Bands and cheered us on), but apparently not.

'Sorry, Mini-Rafferty,' she said. 'I don't make the rules.'

'But couldn't you bend them for me?' I said.

'Nope,' she said. 'I'm a very serious part-time volunteer librarian.'

Fair enough, I suppose, but I do feel there should be some advantages to being the sister of the best friend of a part-time volunteer librarian. Anyway, I got out three books, so at least I have some decent entertainment to console me for having to not only go back to school, but spend all day listening to Vanessa go on and on about how she's going to be 'the face of Bluebird Bakery Yummy Scrummy Cookies'.

Cass, by the way, is totally convinced that Vanessa is going to get the job.

'The thing about Vanessa,' she said, when we were walking down Griffith Avenue on our way home, 'is that, even though she's a bit deluded, she's not totally deluded. At least when it comes to her acting skills. Maybe she actually was amazing at her audition.'

'Maybe she was,' I said. 'But she is still a bit ... unreliable.' When we'd last seen Vanessa, she was in the cloakroom telling some unsuspecting second year that she was a professional actress, which is a barefaced lie because she hasn't got that job (yet) and she's definitely never done any professional work before. 'And remember when she was totally sure that theatrical agents were going to come to the summer camp and sign her up?'

'I know,' said Cass. 'But I'm telling you, I have a feeling she's going to be in that ad. It'd just be our luck to have to put up with Vanessa on our tellies as well as at school.'

'And on posters too,' I said. 'Don't forget the posters.'

Vanessa isn't the only one around here who is confident about a future in showbiz. Tonight Mum and Dad's musical society held their auditions for their next production, *My Fair Lady*. Their last show, *Oliver!*, was a big success, not least because Dad took over one of the lead roles at the last minute and, to my great surprise, he was totally brilliant.

Anyway, their old director has had to take a break from the musical society for a while because of some work thing so now they have a new director. She was just the assistant director last time and apparently she wants to put on quite a spectacular show. After Dad's amazing performance in the summer, he is sure he is going to get another big part. Well, he won't admit it, but I know it's what he's thinking. Every time I ask him about it, he gets all bashful and says things like, 'Oh, it's up to the director, there are lots of good people in the musical society', but there's a strangely confident look on his face that says, 'I know they will remember my triumphant performance as the Beadle!'

In fairness, he's probably right to be confident. I still can't believe what a good dancer he turned out to be. It seems quite unfair that neither Rachel nor I have inherited his amazing dancing skills. And he can jump into the air and click his heels to the side too! It's really impressive. I've been trying for years and I still can't do that. And I only weigh half as much as him, so you'd think I'd be a bit more nimble.

WEDNESDAY ❀

How come I am only fifteen years old and already have not one nemesis, but two? And both of them are younger than me! First of all, of course, there's Daisy's terrible baby. I know Mum thinks it's impossible for a baby to hate another person, but literally every single time I've met that baby it's yelled and puked on me, and if that doesn't show hatred I don't know what does. And now, with the headbutting, it's resorted to physical violence! God knows what it'll do when it's actually big enough to, like, attack me properly. At least at the moment I can easily escape it because it's too young to crawl after me. And of course, apart from the headbutting (and I'll watch out for that in future), it can't do any serious damage yet. I mentioned this to Rachel after dinner today, and she laughed and laughed in a callous way.

'I bet that baby could take you in a fight now if it really tried,' she said. 'You're pretty weedy, really.'

A bit much coming from her – she's hardly the pinnacle of physical fitness. I'd say she's about as scrawny and feeble as I am.

Anyway, luckily I don't see the baby very often. But I do have to see my other nemesis, that horrible little Sorcha Mulligan. I haven't written about her in a while because she and her mysteriously normal parents (how did they produce such a monster?) have been on holiday, but I was doing my homework in my room this evening (yes, we've started getting proper serious homework again) and when I looked up at the window, there she was in her own room across the road, staring at me! Her traditional activity is to make horrible faces at me and dance around, but this evening she just stared at me for ages in a genuinely spooky way. I actually started feeling a bit scared after a while. I don't know how she managed to stare so long without blinking. It was really creepy.

Mum always says I should just ignore her and it's silly to let a seven-year-old child annoy me so much, but I bet if I hovered outside Mum's study window and just stared at her like a terrifying serial killer/ghost child it would do her head in too.

On the plus side, a year ago Karen Rodgers was my nemesis – she was pretty awful to me when Mum's book about a teenager came out and everyone thought it was about me – but she's calmed down now and never really bothers me at all. Not directly, I mean. She still irritates me by going on about her drama group and her amazing boyfriend Bernard the Fairytale Prince (we call him this because she met him when he was being a fairytale prince at Vanessa's birthday party). But she's not actively trying to annoy me when she does this, so I can't really call her my nemesis anymore.

That does still leave the baby and the Mulligan kid, though. I think the baby might be innately violent, but maybe the little Mulligan will find something better to do than freak me out? There must be something she likes doing besides harassing her neighbours. Mustn't there?

THURSDAY ◎

God, school really is more boring this year. Even Miss Kelly telling us about natural disasters and the awful environmental consequences of leaving the water running while you're brushing your teeth can't make things exciting. And of course, we were right, all the teachers are constantly going on about how this is a big exam year. You'd think we were doing our college finals or something.

The only plus side is that Mrs O'Reilly seems to have forgotten that she banned me and Cass from sitting next to each other in history, so once again I can amuse myself by drawing pictures of Cass in the guise of historical figures and taunting her with them. Childish I know, but I have to take my pleasures where I can find them. I did a very good picture of her as Queen Victoria today, right under Mrs O'Reilly's nose.

Home isn't much more exciting than school. When my parents aren't pointlessly reminding me and Rachel about our exams (which, lest we forget, are not for another nine months. Well, almost), they are blathering on about *My Fair Lady*. Dad is constantly singing 'I'm Getting Married in the Morning'. I tried playing my snare drum earlier this evening to drown him out, but it didn't work because he has a very booming voice.

And to make matters worse, when I was doing this Mum came into my room and told me to stop making so much noise! I told her I wasn't making half as much noise as Dad, which was perfectly true, but she told me not to be silly and walked out before I could say anything else. I wish they wouldn't treat me like a baby. They can't go on about how I'm doing these supposedly really important exams one minute and then talk to me like I'm the same age as Sorcha Mulligan the next.

Right, I'm going to go and read more of *I Capture the Castle* now. It is very good. It's about a teenage girl with a spoiled older sister who is very bored with her life and who sits there just praying for something exciting to happen. And then it does. I can really relate to it, even though she lives in a castle in the middle of the English countryside in the 1930s and I live in a semi-detached house in Drumcondra in the twenty-first century.

FRIDAY ⌣

Nothing much happened in school today, apart from Vanessa going on about her future advertising stardom.

'Don't worry, girls,' she said to me and Cass when she was leaving school today. 'I won't forget about you once I'm on TV.'

I hope she does. Maybe she'd stop talking to us then.

What makes her bragging even more ridiculous is the fact that she hasn't even heard back from the agency yet. I'm starting to hope this means she hasn't got the job. But I bet she has. I just have a feeling. So does Cass. She and Alice came over to my house after school to make our famous delicious fudge. We've started regretfully to accept that our dream of becoming the youngest celebrity chefs ever might be a bit ambitious, or possibly even deluded, but we might as well keep our hand in.

'We can't take our eye off the ball,' said Cass, as we mixed together the ingredients. 'Someone else might step in and become the first teenage sweet-making sensation. Plus we can still sell the fudge at our gigs. Or give it away as a gimmick if people aren't willing to pay for it.'

'If Vanessa gets that ad,' I said, passing her some bits of white chocolate (we were experimenting with a new flavour), 'she'll steal our thunder. Well, sort of.'

'Not "sort of" at all!' cried Cass. 'It's an ad for biscuits! We make fudge! And besides, it's not as though she makes the biscuits herself.'

'Oh God, listen to us,' I said. 'We're talking as if she's got it already. We still don't know whether she has or not. And I'm still hoping not.'

'I'm kind of sure she has, though,' said Cass.

'I'm not,' said Alice. 'It's not that she isn't talented, but there are loads of talented girls out there. There's no guarantee that she'll get the job.'

'I'm sure she's got it,' I said, absent-mindedly eating one of the nuts for the next batch of fudge. 'Unfortunately.'

'Maybe we're psychic,' said Cass. 'Actually, if we were, we

35

really would definitely get our own cooking show.'

'Psychic teenage chefs,' I said. 'Imagine the theme tune.'

'What on earth are you waffling on about now?' said Rachel, coming into the kitchen.

'Our future amazing TV career,' I said. 'Leave that white chocolate alone! We don't have a lot of it.'

'I was just tasting it,' said Rachel.

'Well, don't hover over us,' I said. 'We're trying a new recipe and we need to concentrate.'

Rachel looked very insulted.

'I have no desire to hover over you, thanks very much,' she said. 'I'm going out.'

She and Tom and Jenny and a bunch of their friends are all going to one of their friend's band's gigs. She says she's got to go out while she can because Mum and Dad have really started going on at her about the fact that it's her Leaving Cert year. In fact, I must admit that for once they are being tougher on her than they have been on me. Soon she'll barely be able to go out at all. So I suppose I can't begrudge her her freedom now.

Anyway, both batches of the fudge turned out very well, especially the white chocolate one. When I think back to how bad the first lot we made was, it's kind of amazing how much we've improved. A bit like the band.

And speaking of which, we've got a practice tomorrow. It's still just out in Alice's garage, but fingers crossed we'll hear from Veronica soon about the practice space and then we won't have to trek all the way out to Kinsealy just to practise for an hour. Of course, Alice will have to trek into town, but she doesn't mind as much because it'll mean she'll be able to meet Richard more easily afterwards. So it's an excellent situation all round. In the meantime, I hope my parents can give me and Cass a lift tomorrow – Cass's parents are going to one of her brother's boring football matches so they can't.

SATURDAY ☺

Very good band practice this afternoon, and definitely worth the epic journey out to Alice's place (I got the bus because my parents were going to look at plants in some stupid garden centre with Maria who lives around the corner, so they couldn't give me a lift). We now have eight whole songs of our own that we can play pretty well from start to finish, as well as a few covers like the Kinks song we sang at the Battle of the Bands last year. But we don't spend much time on the covers anymore, because it's much more fun to play our own. All those songwriting workshops in the summer camp were really useful. Though in a way the most useful thing of all has been my rhyming dictionary, which has made it so much easier to write song lyrics. I'd never have thought of rhyming 'long ago' with 'pistachio' (it's in a song about my memories of Paperboy) if it wasn't for that.

SUNDAY ☼

Mum and Dad have always said that Dublin is like a village and that you can't walk down the street without seeing someone you know. I always thought this was ridiculous because (a) Dublin is clearly a large city and (b) there have been plenty of times when I have wanted to bump into people and didn't, like when I really fancied Paperboy, and Cass and I would go for walks around the neighbourhood hoping we would see him. If Dublin really was like a village we'd have definitely caught a glimpse of him at some stage. I mean, he only lived two miles away.

But anyway, sometimes it really does feel like a village because last week we met not one but two Paulas and today

I went into town with Cass and Alice and we met even more summer-camp people. It was almost like being back there again. We were coming down Grafton Street when we saw them. There was Sam, who doesn't technically count as a summer-camp person because we first met him when we were doing the school musical – he was playing Uncle Albert in *Mary Poppins*. But we only really got to know him during the summer. He was with his comics-writing partner Lucy and also with Gemma, who did the drama part of the summer camp and had to put together a play with Karen and Vanessa (and our friend Jane).

Of course we all stopped for a chat. It was great to see them, but actually I did feel a bit odd about the whole thing because the last time I saw Gemma and Sam together, they were snogging in front of the stage at the end-of-camp disco thing. I've seen Sam once since the camp ended, but Gemma wasn't there and I didn't want to ask, at the time, if anything was going on between them. But now it looks like there might be. I mean, they weren't hugely close during the camp, but now they're clearly meeting up in town at the weekends. So I presume something is happening.

Not that I care, of course. Sam is definitely not my type. His hair's light brown, for one thing. I generally only like boys with darker hair. He's really nice though. We always had really good conversations about books. Actually, I think I still have a book belonging to him somewhere. He's one of those people I wish I saw more often. I hope Gemma doesn't mess him around. I don't really know her that well, but she always seemed pretty nice. We didn't stay talking to them for long because Cass and I were walking Alice to her bus stop and her bus only goes once an hour so we couldn't miss it. But we said we'd organise a proper meet-up in town soon, which is cool.

After we'd said goodbye and were walking past Trinity on our way to the bus stop, Cass said, 'Well, well, well. Sam and Gemma!'

'What about them?' said Alice.

'It looks like that close encounter at the disco wasn't a one-off,' said Cass, like she was some sort of gossip show presenter.

'Hmm, I suppose so,' said Alice. 'What do you think, Bex?'

'Oh yeah, I think they must be,' I said. 'Going out I mean. Or something. Something's going on. Good luck to them. I mean, they're both really nice. '

Cass and Alice looked at me a bit strangely, but Cass just said, 'Yeah, they are. And remember, Gemma managed to put together a play with Vanessa and Karen without running amok and killing either of them. So she must be a very together person.'

Then we stopped talking about Gemma and started talking about what Vanessa's ad might be like (look, we're talking as if she's definitely got it already). Alice suggested that Vanessa might have to dress up like an actual chocolate chip cookie, which wouldn't be so bad as she would look ridiculous and she mightn't boast about it so much. Then Cass said that it could be an animated ad, and that Vanessa might only be doing a voiceover.

'Which would obviously be the best result of all,' she said, and Alice and I agreed.

Though then Alice said, 'Aren't we thinking too much about this? I mean, why do we care so much about Vanessa's ad? We should just ignore her.'

And she's right, of course. But still. It's very hard to ignore Vanessa when we have to put up with her every day.

LATER

If something really was going on between Sam and Gemma, wouldn't they have been on their own? Though I suppose I go into town with just Cass and Liz quite often, and they are definitely going out. Oh well, it hasn't got anything to do with me.

MONDAY ☼

Well, it looks like Cass and I really are psychic (possibly) because of course Vanessa did get that part in the ad, which is yet more proof that there is no such thing as karma. If there was, then Vanessa would currently be living under a bridge like a troll. The ad people rang her this morning, as Cass and I discovered as soon as we walked into our form room to dump things in our lockers. She was holding forth to the whole class, who were, for once, actually standing around her, actively listening. They really shouldn't encourage her like that.

'The contract is just for one television advertisement and poster campaign,' Vanessa was saying when we came in. 'But if the campaign is as successful as they're sure it will be, then there's going to be, like, a whole series of different ads all based on my character, Kookie.'

Kookie! The mind reels.

'I'm sure there will be,' said Caroline, who seems to be as

loyal to Vanessa as ever.

'They're already working on follow-up ideas,' said Vanessa smugly.

Good grief. So we might have to put up with her on our tellies for years on end. And on billboards. What a terrible prospect.

Alice, however, is more optimistic.

'Maybe it won't be too bad,' she said at lunchtime. 'I mean, we do know she's a good actress. Maybe she'll be playing a likeable character? The ad could be really good!'

I suppose this is possible, but still. First of all, the character is called Kookie, which doesn't bode well. And second of all, I don't actually care how good the ads are. When I am at home I want to forget about the irritating elements of school. I don't want to be reminded of Vanessa in the ad breaks of *Laurel Canyon*.

But at least there are no billboards between school and my house so I won't have to look at any posters of her every day. And – this really is good news – we all got texts from Veronica this evening saying the Knitting Factory scheme is definitely going ahead! Hurrah! She said it should be up and running in about two weeks and before then she's going to send us links to the venue's registration website so we can book workshops and studio time online. I just hope all our parents don't get weird about the whole Junior Cert thing and stop us going there. Surely they can't begrudge us a few hours a week for our creative hobby? I mean, it's not like we'd be going there for wild nights out, just a couple of hours every weekend in the middle of the afternoon. What else could we be doing then? After all, there's only so much studying we can do. And I know Mum did piano lessons until she was in college, so she managed to do her exams AND go to music lessons every week. Band practice is basically the same thing, isn't it? Just a bit more social.

TUESDAY ☾

My parents have just come home from their musical rehearsal. They weren't singing when they came in, as they usually do, so at first I was worried that Dad hadn't got a part at all and was too sad to sing. But it turns out that not only does he have a part, he has the lead! He's playing Henry Higgins, who decides to teach the flower seller Eliza Doolittle to be a posh lady. Rachel and I were impressed when we heard the news.

'The actual lead!' I said. 'That's brilliant. Well done!'

'Why don't you look more cheerful about it?' said Rachel.

But it turns out that Dad didn't actually want the lead! He wanted to play Eliza's dad, Alfred the dustman, because, Dad says, he 'does lots of dancing' and Dad wanted to 'let those skilled feet fly'. And Henry Higgins doesn't dance at all. In fact, now I come to think of it, he doesn't even sing much either – I've seen the film and he just sort of speaks over the music (not in a rapping way, it's not that sort of musical). So even though Dad is meant to be feeling all honoured, he is actually very disappointed because he was looking forward to prancing all over the stage.

A part of me thinks he's being a bit ungrateful – after all, when they started the last production he was just an under-study and member of the chorus, and now he's got a huge part – but I have to admit that it does seem like a bit silly of the new director to put their finest dancer (which he really is, I know it sounds mad) in a part where he won't have to dance. It would be like asking me to join a band and then expecting me to sing instead of play the drums. Mum was trying to cheer him up and kept saying that his stage cha-risma makes him perfect for Henry Higgins, but I heard her on the phone later telling her friend Maria that she didn't know what the new director was thinking, and that Joe, the man who's playing Albert, isn't half as good as Dad at dancing and singing.

'He'd have been perfectly suited for Henry Higgins,' said Mum. 'I do think they're wasting Ed.'

Poor Dad. As for Mum, she doesn't have a main part. She is one of the senior chorus members and apparently she is playing a sort of cheeky Edwardian flower seller in the market and pub scenes. She was a saucy tavern wench in their production of *Oliver!*, so I hope she isn't getting typecast. But she is also playing a posh lady at the races and a few other things, as well as being an understudy for Henry Higgins's housekeeper, so hopefully she won't spend the entire thing half naked (well, wearing a very low-cut dress) like last time.

I have finished *I Capture the Castle*. I loved it and I cried at the end. Now I am reading *Code Name Verity* which is brilliant in a very different way. And it is making me count my blessings. I may have annoying parents, but at least I'm not in France being tortured by Nazis. So things could be worse.

WEDNESDAY ❦

It's a sorry state of affairs when the most dramatic thing

happening in my life is Vanessa telling us about her stupid ad campaign. Apparently, she has wardrobe fittings and a rehearsal after school today because they are going to start making it very soon. She has been sent a copy of the script, but she can't reveal any details yet (she shouldn't even have told us her character's ridiculous name because it is all meant to be top secret). Anyway, I'm very glad she can't tell us all about the ad because it's going to be bad enough having to watch it when it actually airs without getting a blow-by-blow account of it before it's even been on telly.

'All I'll say is,' she declared at lunchtime, while we all tried to pay no attention to her, 'that you'll all be saying my catchphrase in a few weeks!'

I can guarantee that I will not be doing this.

And that's not even the worst bit. Apparently, there will also be a song. Sung by Vanessa.

'They might even release it as a single,' she said.

'Bernard and I will buy one each,' said Karen.

Words fail me. That's all we need, Vanessa on our radios as well as our tellies.

Oh, I feel so blah. Not about Vanessa, though she doesn't help my mood. I just keep remembering that this time last year was when everything started to happen. First of all, I met

Paperboy. It was around this week of September that he first called at our house to collect the money for delivering the newspapers on Saturdays. And then soon after that I got my drums, and we started Hey Dollface. So much was going on a year ago!

Oh my God. I've just realised something.

I got my drums a year ago.

Which means ...

I can't believe I haven't thought of this before now. I got my drums from a friend of Tom's called Sam (to distinguish him from musical/summer-camp Sam, I will call him Drummer Sam) because he was moving to America for a year. But now that year is up! Why hasn't Rachel – or indeed Tom – mentioned it to me yet? Maybe he's forgotten all about his drums (though I know I wouldn't if I'd left them with someone else for a year). Or maybe he's not coming back.

Oh God, I don't know what to do. Obviously the sensible thing to do is just ask Rachel to ask Tom. But what if Sam actually has forgotten about his drums, but this reminds him of them and he decides he wants them back? Is it better to just say nothing and hope he forgets all about it? I think that's what I will do. It's just like that proverb about letting sleeping dogs (or drum owners) lie.

THURSDAY ◎

I can't stop worrying about the drums. I keep expecting Rachel to say something about Drummer Sam and how he's back from America and can't wait to start playing the drums again. Obviously, I know they are his drums and he has a perfect right to have them back, but it's been so long since he went away that I'd almost forgotten they belonged to him and weren't actually mine. Could he actually have forgotten about them? I can't imagine I'd forget about owning an entire drum kit, but maybe living in America was so exciting it drove all thoughts of drumming out of his mind. After all, when Paperboy moved to Canada he seemed to forget all about his old Dublin life and didn't contact me for weeks on end. Maybe going to North America does something to boys' minds?

Not that I'm bitter about Paperboy. Seriously, I'm really not. I genuinely like hearing from him these days and I am definitely not still pining for him like I was at the beginning of the year. Though I have to say that I'm glad he has never mentioned a girlfriend to me. I think I would still feel very weird about that, even though I went out with John Kowalski. Which may be hypocritical of me, but is still true.

Anyway, thinking about Paperboy isn't going to help with this drum-kit situation. I haven't mentioned it to Cass and Alice because I'm pretty sure they would just tell me to get Rachel to ask Tom about it, which I still can't bear to do in case Drummer Sam actually has forgotten about them, in which case it's surely better not to remind him.

I keep looking at my (or rather, as I have to keep telling myself, Drummer Sam's) snare drum, which is the smallest drum and the only bit of the drum kit I keep at home rather than in Alice's garage. What would happen to Hey Dollface if I had no drums? I know there'll be a kit at the new practice space, but that wouldn't be the same and I wouldn't be able to take any of it home. And practising on the snare at home is the only reason I'm halfway decent at the drums now. I can't afford to get a whole kit of my own. Or even just a snare really.

I will just keep my fingers crossed and hope Drummer Sam forgets about it all.

FRIDAY ☺

I had a dream about the drums last night. I was out in Alice's place and I couldn't find them anywhere. Cass and Alice were both playing their instruments, but I was just wandering around looking for my drums. I can't stop worrying about them; it's in the back of my mind all the time. I forget about it while I'm doing normal things like walking to school with Cass or listening to Mrs Harrington (who is still quite quiet and distracted) talk about poetry or Miss Kelly talk about what will happen to the world food supply if bees become extinct, but, every so often, I remember it and feel a little bit sick.

Anyway, I was distracted from drum dreams when I got to school by Vanessa's dramatic new haircut. She is filming the ad tomorrow and she got it cut into a fringe just for the shoot! Apparently, the directors felt a fringe was 'an integral part of the character'. She says she could have worn a wig, but she wanted to go all the way.

'A true actress always fully commits to her role,' she declared.

I am almost impressed by this. I don't know if I'd have dared get my hair cut in a new way just for a part in an ad, not after the traumatic hair disaster I've had this year. Vanessa really is taking the job very seriously. And I hate to admit it, but the fringe does suit her. Unlike my own fringe, which went all fluffy and ridiculous as soon as it got wet (it really is growing out at last, thank God). Vanessa's fringe is quite sleek and well behaved.

Not that I said any of this to her, of course. I'm not going to encourage her egomania. Anyway, Karen and Caroline were gushing enough for all of us.

'You're so brave, Vanessa,' said Karen, as if Vanessa had agreed to go into a war zone or a burning building or something. 'I don't know if I could do something so dramatic, even if it was for such a serious role.'

'And it looks amazing too,' said Caroline.

I noticed Alison wasn't taking part in this fawning fest, though. In fact, she wasn't even sitting with Karen, Vanessa and Caroline. She was on the other side of the room talking to Emma about computer coding instead. The two of them both want to do some sort of coding course for secondary-school students that's starting at the teacher-training college down the road from our school. Emma says it will take her one step closer to her dream of creating computers that can think for themselves. Of course, that's not what the people who are running the course say it will do, but Emma is pretty convinced she's going to make a breakthrough soon.

Anyway, it was good to see Alison breaking away from her usual gang. If only Caroline would do the same. But she seems happy enough telling Vanessa how wonderful she is. I don't know how she does it. It's not like Vanessa is particularly nice to her (or anyone). Maybe Vanessa actually pays her to be her sidekick? It's the only thing that makes sense.

SATURDAY ☺

Met Jane today. She knows all about Vanessa's ad because of her mum being friends with Vanessa's mother. That's how they ended up going to the same drama and dance class last year. Anyway, Vanessa's mother is very enthusiastic about the ad and she told Mrs Park it was a pity Jane didn't have Vanessa's drive and ambition! Which just shows the apple doesn't fall far from the obnoxious tree.

'I wish you had auditioned for that ad instead of Vanessa,' I said. 'You're just as good at acting and singing as she is. And you have the advantage of not being a crazed egomaniac, so you'd be much nicer to work with. If I'd talked to both you and Vanessa for two minutes and I had to decide which of you would get a job, I would definitely choose you.'

'It's very nice of you to say so,' said Jane. 'But actually, I don't think I'd want to be in an ad anyway. I mean, imagine if it turned out to be for something you really didn't like? If it was for food, first of all you'd probably have to eat lots of it, which would be horrible. And then the ad would be on telly and everyone would associate you with whatever it was for, for years and years. It's more trouble than it's worth.'

'I suppose,' I said. 'This is for Bluebird Bakery biscuits, though, remember? And they genuinely are nice.'

'There's only so many biscuits you can eat without getting sick,' said Jane wisely. 'I bet Vanessa will be sick of them by the time they've finished making this ad. Just imagine, she might never be able to eat a biscuit again. Anyway, I'd much prefer to work on my own acting things. I think I'd like to start my own theatre company.'

'What, right now?' I said, surprised. I know Jane is very talented, but starting a whole theatre company does seem like a lot of work for someone who's still at school, especially during Junior Cert year.

'No!' said Jane. 'In the future. Eventually. If I don't find something else I like doing more first. But it would be really cool to put plays together with a bunch of other people.' She looked at me. 'You could write something for us.'

'You're sounding a bit like John Kowalski,' I said, and she looked so appalled I burst out laughing. 'I was joking! It's just he had a big plan for becoming a famous writer-actor person. And he was always telling me to write stuff. But he

54

only wanted me to write stuff he thought was cool.'

'Well, I'd want you to write whatever you like,' said Jane.

'Alright, then,' I said. 'I'll have a think about it.'

'Well, you've got plenty of time,' said Jane. 'I don't think I'll have a theatre company for at least, I dunno, five years.'

I actually would like to try writing a play. I mean, if John could do it, I bet I could too. And I bet mine would be more entertaining than his. After all, he didn't believe writing should have jokes in it.

Anyway, later I mentioned to Jane that I'd seen Lucy, Sam and Gemma. She was in the same group as Gemma, Vanessa and Karen at the summer camp and I was pretty sure they'd have stayed in touch.

'Is there anything going on between them?' I said. 'Sam and Gemma, I mean. Not Lucy.'

'I'm actually not sure,' said Jane. 'I know Gemma fancied him during the summer camp ...'

'Did she really?' I said. 'I had no idea.'

'Yeah,' said Jane. 'She was actually a bit jealous of you, because you and Sam got on so well! She said she wished she had as much to talk to him about as you did.'

'Oh!' I said. I felt a bit funny. 'Well, I hope she knew there was no reason to be jealous.'

'Well, I told her that at the time,' said Jane. 'I knew you didn't fancy him.' She paused. 'You didn't, did you?'

'God, no!' I said. 'Of course not! So what happened between them? After the disco?'

'Not much, I think,' said Jane. 'So far. She was away with her family for a few weeks – that's why she wasn't at that meet-up we had after the camp, remember?'

'Oh yeah,' I said. That was the only time I've seen Sam since the camp ended.

'Anyway, I haven't seen Gemma myself since school started,' Jane went on. 'So I don't really know what the story is. But I was going to message her to tell her about Vanessa's ad so maybe I could ask a subtle question ...'

'Well, if they're actually going out I'm sure she'll tell you anyway,' I said. And then Jane realised it was time for both of us to go home for dinner and we didn't talk about Gemma and Sam again.

I don't really know why I'm thinking about it now. I mean, I asked myself in the summer whether I liked Sam in that way and I decided I didn't. Maybe I'm just becoming bitter and I don't want to hear about anyone finding love? That's a bit sad and depressing.

SUNDAY ☼

I can't believe my parents have the nerve to give out to me whenever I play my tiny little snare drum very, very quietly. I was woken up today at half seven by the sound of my dad singing about the rain in Spain falling mainly in the plain at top volume. He's never quiet in the mornings at the best of times, but this was particularly bad. I put my fingers in my ears and tried to ignore the noise and go back to sleep, but it didn't work. Rachel stayed in Jenny's last night, so she wasn't going to do anything about it. It was up to me. Eventually, I staggered out of my room and asked him very politely and sensibly to be a tiny bit quieter.

'What are you doing?' I cried. 'Why are you up so early?'

Dad looked surprised.

'It's nearly eight o'clock!' he said.

'It's half seven!' I said. 'On a Sunday!'

'Sorry, love,' said Dad, looking a bit guilty, as well he might. 'I just want to try and give Henry Higgins a bit more ... oomph before we have the next rehearsal. You know. A bit more razzle dazzle.'

'I don't think anyone needs that much oomph,' I said

grumpily. 'Or razzle dazzle. Especially at this time of the morning.'

There was no chance of me getting back to sleep again so I just stayed up, even though I really wanted a lie-in. On the plus side, Dad was very apologetic about waking me up, and even made us both a delicious fry-up breakfast. While we were eating it, he said he wants to make Henry Higgins a 'less restrained' character. I have a feeling this means he's going to insist on putting in some dance moves. I hope the director doesn't mind.

MONDAY ☺

So Vanessa's ad shoot went brilliantly. At least, that's what she said. Constantly. All day.

'They'd never met a beginner who was such a professional before,' she said.

She didn't even shut up during class, even after Frau O'Hara gave out to her in German (in German class and also in the German language. Though Vanessa didn't seem to understand any of it, so Frau O'Hara had to say it all again in English). Anyway, apparently Vanessa's song (which she recorded separately to the filming) sounds amazing and we will all love it. She keeps telling us this. Maybe she thinks that if she says it often enough she can brainwash us. It will not work on me. Anyway, we'll get to hear it in all its glory in just a few weeks. I am not exactly counting the seconds.

But now to more important matters than Vanessa's ad. I finally gave in and told Alice and Cass about my drum fears. I think it was because I had another dream about my drums last night. I was trying to study and there was a terrible ominous booming and I looked up and saw Miss Kelly was playing my bass drum in my bedroom! She kept staring at me while banging the drum. It was surprisingly sinister.

I told Cass and Alice about Drummer Sam's impending return at lunch today. The weather was really lovely and the three of us were sitting out in the playing fields. Cass and Alice were talking about whether we should paint a Hey Dollface logo on the front of the drum kit and the more they talked about it, the worse I felt and FINALLY they noticed that I hadn't said anything in a while and (as Alice said later) looked like I was going to get sick.

'Are you all right, Bex?' asked Alice.

'Sorry, what?' I said.

'Are you actually listening to us?' asked Cass. 'We were

talking about the very important issue of drum logos.'

'Sorry,' I said again. And then I sighed. I knew I couldn't keep it to myself anymore. 'I'm just worried about something. Something drum-related.'

'What?' said Alice.

'Are you okay?' said Cass.

I took another deep breath.

'Okay,' I said. 'There is a chance – a tiny chance. Or actually maybe a big chance. I don't actually know. Anyway, there is a chance I might lose my drums. I mean, I might have to give them back to the friend of Tom's who lent them to me.'

At first, Cass and Alice were quite upset, but once I'd reminded them of the full situation, Alice said what I'd been afraid she would say.

'But why don't you just ask Rachel to ask Tom to ask Drummer Sam?' she said. 'At least you'd know.'

I explained about the whole 'let sleeping dogs lie' thing, but, as I had feared, Alice and Cass weren't impressed.

'You really should just ask her,' said Alice. 'I do understand why you haven't, but you have to do it at some stage. I mean, if you don't have drums, we'll have to sort something else out for the band.'

'Yeah,' said Cass. 'And the sooner we know, the sooner we

can sort something out.'

'I know, I know,' I said, and I do. Of course they are right. If my drums (okay, Drummer Sam's drums) are going to be taken away from me, I need to come up with a contingency plan, but there is a part of me that just doesn't want to deal with it at all. Which is pathetic, I know, but I can't help it. Anyway, I have decided that I will ask Rachel about it on Saturday. Which gives me four whole days to pysche myself up.

TUESDAY ☾

Maybe it is a sign of my advanced age, or maybe it's because I'm trying to distract myself from the thought of (possibly) losing my drums, but I keep thinking how long it's been since big things happened. I just realised that today it's five months exactly since I kissed someone. And by someone, of course, I mean John Kowalski. I know he turned out to be a terrible person, but he was a very good kisser. In fact, if I'm being perfectly honest, he was a better kisser than Paperboy. I would never have admitted that at the time, but it's true.

Anyway, it feels like a lot longer than five months. I really do know, in my heart of hearts, that I'll kiss someone else some day, but right now I feel quite sad. I don't really know why. I just found myself listening to music that reminded me of back in March and April, when we were doing the musical and me and John got together, and it's got me feeling weirdly nostalgic for the whole thing. Just thinking of the way he called me 'Rafferty' still makes me feel a bit funny. But I must make myself remember how he used to go on about himself all the time, and how he tried to make me write serious things when I wanted to write funny things, and how he let all of us down about the musical. Being a (very) good kisser doesn't make up for that.

LATER

My parents have just come home from their musical rehearsal.

'How did it go?' I asked. I was thinking of Dad's attempts to 'oomph' up Henry Higgins.

'Pretty well,' said Dad cheerfully. 'I think we're really getting somewhere already! The director seems very open to my ideas.'

'Wow, that's great,' I said.

I noticed Mum had rather a strange expression on her face.

'How about you, Mother dear?' I asked, like the good daughter I am.

'Toiling away in the chorus,' she said, but she seemed pretty cheerful about it.

'Did you oomph up your role as a flower seller?' I said.

'What?' said Mum.

'Dad said he was going to oomph up Henry Higgins!' I said.

'Ah,' said Mum. 'Well, he certainly did that.'

She says she didn't need to do much to her flower-selling role as it already involves quite a lot of prancing around and strolling sassily.

'It's got lots of oomph already,' she said.

Anyway, they both seem pretty happy about the show, which is good. At least it meant they forgot to ask me pointless, boring questions about how much studying I'd done (the answer is of course none, because my exams are not for nearly nine months, but I did do all my homework nice and early).

WEDNESDAY ❁

We have booked our studio time in the Knitting Factory! The

registration site went live today and Veronica sent us all links. They won't start having workshops for a month or so, but the studios are going to be available the week after next, and Hey Dollface will be rocking out there on Saturday week for two hours. I can't wait. It'll be like being back in the summer camp again, except slightly colder because it's the end of September, not July. They are also going to open up those art studios in the Knitting Factory complex, so maybe Sam and Lucy, and Ellie from school, and people will come along too.

It still doesn't take away my drum worries, though. I really will have to ask Rachel on Saturday, I can't take this stress for much longer.

THURSDAY ◎

I have drums! I mean, I can keep the drums! Oh, I feel so relieved. It's like a big drum-shaped weight has been taken off my shoulders. We had just sat down to dinner (sausage casserole, one of my favourites) and Rachel said, 'Oh yeah, Bex, I meant to tell you. I heard from Tom's friend Sam today.'

My stomach sank to the floor. I couldn't say anything.

'You remember Sam, right?' said Rachel. 'The original

owner of your drums?'

'Yeah, of course I do,' I said. 'How is he? Does he, um, like America?'

I think I sounded completely normal, but really I was just thinking, 'This is it. He wants his drums back.'

'He's grand,' said Rachel. 'He loves it there. But he's not coming back. I mean, I presume he will eventually. But his mum's been offered a permanent job and it looks like they're all staying in New York. He's talking about going to college in America too and everything. He wants to go to Yale.'

'Oh,' I said. I took a deep breath. 'So does he want me to send his drums over there? I don't really know how we'd do that. I mean, it would cost a fortune.'

'What?' said Rachel. 'No, of course he doesn't! He told me to tell you that you could keep them for as long as you liked. And ... didn't he lend you some other musical things as well?'

'An amp,' I said. 'And some mikes.'

'Well, you can keep all of it,' said Rachel. 'He says he's producing most of his music on his laptop now, anyway.'

I couldn't believe it. I still can't.

'Wow,' I said. 'That's brilliant. Tell him thanks very much from me!'

'Oh dear, does that mean we have to put up with you

banging away on that small drum forever?' said Mum, but she didn't look too annoyed really.

'Yes,' I said happily.

'Maybe I should tell him to demand them back after all,' said Rachel.

As soon as dinner was finished, I rang Alice and told her the news. This was such important news it had to be told in person rather than in text or IM.

'The band is saved!' I cried.

'Well, it wasn't really in danger,' said Alice sensibly. 'We could have used the drums in the Knitting Factory. But it's very cool.'

'I feel so relieved,' I said. There was a pause on the other end of the phone, and I have a feeling Alice was thinking that I could have avoided the last week of stress if I'd just asked Rachel to get in touch with Sam in the first place. But she didn't say anything about it, because she really is a good and noble friend who never says 'I told you so'. I am not sure I would have been able to resist if that were me. In fact, I feel quite embarrassed by the whole thing myself.

But anyway! Drums forever! I am so happy, even though I now have to write a very boring fake e-mail for German homework about booking a place in a youth hostel.

FRIDAY ☺

I have found out why Mrs Harrington has been so quiet lately. She is writing a book! Apparently, she has been writing for hours every night and is too tired in our classes to do anything but actually teach us, which is fine by me. God knows how much time she wasted last year going on about my mother's books. Usually I am all for teachers wasting time talking about other things besides the subject we're meant to be studying, but not when they're raving about my mother. Though of course Mrs Harrington hasn't forgotten about Mum, because she is her great inspiration!

It all came out at the end of class today. I was walking out of Room 7 and looking forward to eating my ham and salad sandwich when Mrs Harrington said, 'How's your mammy's writing coming along, Rebecca?'

Sadly, I couldn't ignore her, so I said, 'Oh, fine.' And then I thought of something that might cheer Mrs Harrington up. 'She's finished writing the book with Patricia Alexandra Harrington in it!'

Months ago, in a moment of madness, I told Mrs Harrington (whose full name is Patricia Alexandra Harrington) that my mother was going to name a character after her. Of course, then I had to make sure my mother actually did it, which was much easier said than done. But she did it, in the end, so it all worked out, but it was very stressful at the time. Still, all's well that ends well. And Mrs Harrington looked delighted when I mentioned it.

'Oh, I can't wait to read it!' she said. 'Me, in a Rosie Carberry book!'

'Well, just your name,' I reminded her. 'I mean, Patricia Alexandra is the villain.'

'That makes it even more fun,' said Mrs Harrington happily. 'I can't believe my name has inspired your mammy.' Then she looked at me pointedly. 'And actually, she's inspired me!'

'How?' I said nervously. Was Mrs Harrington going to start dressing like my mother in a scary stalker way or something? I wouldn't totally put it past her, given her behaviour in the past.

'I'm writing a book!' said Mrs Harrington.

What is it about my English teachers and writing books? The reason we got Mrs Harrington as an English teacher in the first place was because our original teacher went off to write one! Though she actually had a book deal, which is how she could afford to leave her job. It turns out Mrs Harrington is writing one just for fun and it's all down to, well, you can guess.

'Your mammy made me realise the power of stories,' she said, which is a bit worrying considering she's an English teacher. I would have hoped she'd been aware of the power of stories before she started reading my mother's books. 'And now I want to follow her brilliant example.'

So I presume Mrs Harrington's book is all about a cosy little village with a bakery and a smiling granny and some Irish-dancing kids in it. That more or less sums up most of my mother's books. Then Mrs Harrington told me that she's been working on it for three hours every night, which is pretty impressive. I have never spent so much time on my home-work, even though it's Junior Cert year.

Anyway, I told my mother about it this evening and, to my surprise, she was absolutely delighted.

'Oh, that's wonderful!' she said. 'Tell her I wish her the best of luck.'

I will pass this message on to Mrs Harrington. Maybe she really will become a best-selling author. In fact, maybe she'll become more popular than my mother. Bet Mum wouldn't be so pleased then.

LATER

Before I went to bed, I asked Mum how she would feel if Mrs Harrington became more successful than her by copying her and she just laughed. She has never taken my interest in her career seriously. I don't know why I bother, especially as she reminded me today that the sequel to her teen book about Ruthie O'Reilly will be out in a few months.

'I know the last one took you by surprise,' she said. 'So I thought I'd give you lots of warning.'

The new book is called *Ruthie's Rules for Life* (what a ridiculous title), and Mum swears that she will make it very clear this time that Ruthie has nothing in common with me or Rachel. And she has promised that she has not 'borrowed' any more real-life incidents from our lives. I was hoping she might just not do any interviews at all, but she says that she can't afford to turn down any publicity requests. Anyway, it can't possibly be as bad as the last time. At least I know she's not going to let any newspapers print pictures of me as a kid dancing about in ludicrous pink shorts. I still feel a bit sick when I remember that.

SATURDAY ☺

Oh my God. Something awful has happened. Not to me, and no one has died or been hit by a car or anything, but it's quite awful and I'm kind of surprised at how upset I am. And I still can't totally believe it's true.

Tom broke up with Rachel.

I know! Saint Tom the Perfect Boyfriend! It's shocking. I genuinely thought they would stay together forever and get married or something. Well, maybe not get married – as someone, possibly my mother in one of her rare moments of wisdom, pointed out when Paperboy went off to Canada, most people do not stay with their first boyfriend or girlfriend for the rest of their lives. But I really couldn't imagine them breaking up. I mean, they've been together for nearly two years! I was barely thirteen when they got together and now I'm practically grown up. I just can't believe it. But it's definitely true.

I don't know exactly how or why it happened, or anything like that, because I haven't actually seen Rachel yet. I was in Cass's house this afternoon and stayed there for dinner, so it was quite late when I got home – her mum gave me a lift. As soon as I came in the door, I just sensed something was wrong.

I called 'Hello?' and no one answered, but Mum and Dad were in the kitchen talking quite seriously when I walked in.

'Oh, hi love,' said Mum, in a distracted sort of way. 'I thought I heard someone come in.'

'Is everything okay?' I asked, because she didn't look upset enough for, you know, a sudden death, but she did look a bit stressed. 'Where's Rachel?'

'She's in her room,' said Dad. 'But she's quite upset.'

'About what?' I said, starting to feel nervous. All sorts of things immediately sprang into my mind (though not the actual truth, as it turned out – the thought that Tom might have dumped her didn't even occur to me). What if Rachel had a terrible illness or something? But I knew surely if she did, my parents would look more worried themselves.

Mum and Dad looked at each other.

'It's Tom,' said Mum. 'He's, well, he's broken up with her.'

'Tom?' I said, and I must have kind of shrieked it because Mum immediately went, 'Sssh! Not so loud.'

'But why? How?' I said. I felt stunned, and I still do, really. Tom and Rachel were (and even writing 'were' there looks weird. Like their relationship is now officially in the past) so ... solid. One of those things that never change, like Miss Kelly going on about natural disasters in geography class, only more boring and less scary. I just took them being together for granted. I never actually thought about it much, apart from when Rachel was annoying me (like last week) or when I was feeling bitter after Paperboy went to Canada. Rachel going out with Tom was always just … there. A fixed thing in my world. And now it isn't.

'I don't know any details,' said Mum. 'I just know she was meeting him this afternoon and she came back in a bit of a state.'

'But what did she say?' I said.

'Not much, Bex,' said Dad. 'And we really didn't want to push her. So don't go up to her. She'll talk to us when she's ready.'

'But why?' I said again. An awful thought struck me. 'Is there someone else?'

But they really didn't know anything more. And there wasn't anything I could do. I went upstairs and I was going to knock on the door, but I could hear her crying and it made me feel all weird and awful. I'm used to Rachel being, well, sorted, especially in comparison to me. In fact, sometimes it's kind of annoying, when she's being all wise and sensible. But her being really upset is much worse. I feel terrible for her. I'm almost taking it personally, in a strange way – like, how dare Tom do this to her? Who does he think he is?

Oh God, I can't just ignore her, even if she wants me to. I'm going to go and knock on her door and see what happens.

LATER

Well, not much happened. I could hear Rachel sniffling in there when I knocked on the door, and then the sniffling noises stopped and she said 'Go away!' in a choked-up voice.

'It's me,' I said. 'Are you okay?' I know it was a stupid thing to say because clearly someone who has shut herself up in her room and is still crying is not okay, but I couldn't think of anything else.

'No!' cried Rachel. 'And I don't want to talk to anyone.'

'Oh,' I said. I wasn't exactly surprised. 'Okay. Well, um ... I'm sorry. About ... whatever happened.'

I paused for a second in case she changed her mind and decided she wanted to see me, but she didn't say anything. A second later, she put some sad-sounding music on, so I gave up and came back here. I want to go downstairs and watch telly – there's a good film on tonight – but I feel a bit guilty enjoying myself with my big sister sobbing away upstairs. There's not really anything I can do, though, is there? I feel really rotten. Stupid Tom. So much for him being the perfect boyfriend. I think I might hate him now.

LATER

Is it really wrong that I feel a bit relieved that the whole drum situation was sorted out before this happened? If Tom had broken up with Rachel before then, it would still all be hanging over me. Not that my drumming is as important as Rachel being broken-hearted. But still.

LATER

Oh, it is wrong to feel relieved about any aspect of this. I feel bad for even writing that earlier. Poor Rachel. I can still hear her crying. I hate Tom. I actually do hate him. If he turned up at the house right now, I would hit him, even though that is against all my principles. Well, I wouldn't actually hit him, but I would really want to. How dare he make her feel like this? Horrible smug goon with his stupid perfect presents.

SUNDAY ☼

It's half twelve in the afternoon and there's been no sign of Rachel. I don't think she's even been out to go to the loo, which is a bit worrying. At least, I haven't heard her. Mum says she'll be fine and not to hassle her and that Rachel will come out of her room in her own time, but I heard her sneak upstairs earlier and try to persuade Rachel to come out and have some breakfast. It didn't work though.

Surely hunger will drive her out eventually. When the first really embarrassing picture of me was in the paper last year I refused to come out of my room for ages too. Mum ended up leaving scrambled eggs outside my door in the morning, but that could only keep me going for so long so I eventually ended up having to go downstairs and scavenge for food (actually, I think I just made more scrambled eggs. They're the only things I can cook properly).

Rachel is definitely awake, though, because I heard her talking on the phone earlier. I couldn't hear what she was saying (not that I was eavesdropping or anything), but she sounded upset. I tried knocking on the door again after she got off the phone, but she just yelled at me to go away.

'Come on, Rach,' I said. 'You can talk to me about it. If you want.'

'I don't want to talk to anyone in this house,' she said, and she just put some more loud, sad music on. So I had to give up. I just yelled, 'Well, if you change your mind, you know where I am' over the music and left.

It all feels very wrong. Usually I'm the one being all angsty in my room and she's the one being irritatingly sensible. In theory it should be good to have the tables turned, but it actually just makes me feel sad and weird.

LATER

She finally came out of her room. I actually got a shock when I saw her. She looked awful. I don't mean it in a nasty way. She just looked like she had been really sick. She was very pale and her eyes were all red and sore and her nose was a bit red too. I was in my room when I heard her come out, so I opened my door and peeked out.

'Hey,' I said.

She looked at me and sighed.

'Hey,' she said.

'Are you ...' I began, and then stopped. 'I know you're not okay. Sorry. Tom's a stupid dickhead anyway.'

And I meant it, but I wish I hadn't said anything about Tom, mean or otherwise, because as soon as she heard his name Rachel's face sort of crumpled up and she started to cry. I didn't know what to do because we are not very huggy sort of sisters usually, but I couldn't bear to just stand there watching her cry so I gave her a hug.

'I'm sorry, I'm sorry,' I said into her shoulder. I couldn't think of anything else to say.

'I wish I could think he was a dickhead,' she said. 'But I can't. I just ... I just don't understand anything. I don't know why he did it.'

She sat down on the landing and leaned against her bedroom door. I sat down next to her.

'But what did he say?' I asked.

She took a deep sort of shuddering breath.

'He said he was really sorry, but it didn't feel right anymore,' she said. 'And he couldn't help it.' She rubbed between her brows with her fingers.

'Were there, I dunno, any signs?' I said. 'Looking back?'

'No,' she said. 'Not really. Not at all. I keep thinking there must have been, but I really thought everything was okay.' She looked like she was going to start crying again for a moment, but then she swallowed and went on. 'He just doesn't want to go out with me anymore.'

I couldn't think of anything to say. But then I remembered that she hadn't eaten anything for hours.

'Would you like some toast?' I said.

Rachel looked at me in surprise.

'Um, okay,' she said.

So I went downstairs and made her some toast. When I went back upstairs, she was lying on her bed staring into space and listening to Neil Young singing about everyone going out and having fun while he was sitting at home having none and being lonesome.

'Here you go,' I said, and handed her the toast.

'Thanks,' she said. She took a bite out of it. 'I keep thinking it can't be true,' she said. It was almost as if she was talking to herself. 'I mean, obviously I know it is. True. But I can't totally believe it deep down. I keep thinking he's going to change his mind. Do you think he could?'

I'm not really used to Rachel talking to me like this. Usually it's me who's having some sort of emotional issue and she's the one offering her great advice like a wise woman of the world. So it felt very weird.

'I suppose he could,' I said. 'Maybe he was just having some sort of mental crisis and soon he'll realise it's all been a terrible mistake.'

Rachel sighed.

'Maybe,' she said. 'But ... no, he won't. He seemed pretty sure. Oh God, I don't know.' She looked like she might cry again for a moment. 'Do you mind leaving me on my own for a while?'

'Sure,' I said.

'Thanks for the toast,' she said.

'It's okay,' I said. 'Let me know if you need more food.'

And then I left her, still listening to Neil's wailings. I wish there was something I could do. Maybe Tom really will change his mind? I mean, they seemed so happy together. And I suppose he really was nice, even though he was a bit boring and perfect (though not all that perfect, clearly). And Rachel might sometimes be an annoying big sister, but she's basically a decent person. Why did he change his mind about her? It's not like when I realised what a selfish goon John was. How can you suddenly decide you don't want to go out with someone who is a nice person when you've been with them for so long? It doesn't make any sense.

LATER

I rang Alice (on the landline – I actually feel so rattled by the whole thing that text or IM weren't enough for me) and told her about what happened. She was shocked as well.

'And Rachel really had no idea?' she said.

'She says not,' I said.

'Poor Rachel,' said Alice sadly. 'Maybe we could do something to cheer her up?'

This would be a great idea, but I can't think of anything that would make her more cheerful at the moment. Neither could Alice, really. She eventually suggested writing a song for her, but I don't think that would do the trick. I wrote her one for her birthday and I think she was more amused than touched. But hopefully we'll manage to think of something better.

At least Rachel isn't on her own now. Jenny came round earlier. She's been up in Rachel's room for ages so I hope she'll make her feel better. Or if that's not possible (and I'm afraid it might not be at the moment), at least make her leave her room and have a shower. And eat something. She didn't come down for dinner; she just had more toast instead. Which means she's had nothing but toast for twenty-four hours, and even I couldn't live on that. And I really do love toast.

MONDAY ☼

Rachel didn't want to go to school today, but Mum and Dad were very firm about it.

'I know you're upset, love,' said Mum. 'But you can't hide away from everything.'

'And you can't afford to miss school,' said Dad. 'Not in your Leaving Cert year.'

You'd think that this would be the one time when he could have avoided mentioning the L-word, but I suppose, at this stage, he and Mum are so used to mentioning our stupid exams every five seconds that they don't know how to stop.

'Just one day won't make any difference,' said Rachel, taking a bit of toast (her sole diet for the last few days). But my parents didn't care and sent her off to school. I saw her at lunch – she was surrounded by her mates and I presume everyone is fussing over her. I hope that's what she wants. Knowing Rachel she might prefer if people just left her alone for a while.

Anyway, she got through the day okay without breaking down in floods of tears or running out of the classroom, so that's something, especially when I remember what she was like on Sunday morning. I don't want to sound like my parents, but, to be honest, going to school probably was the best thing she could do. I mean, otherwise she'd just have been at home crying and listening to incredibly miserable music again. And at least she's eating properly now. Mum made a particularly delicious roast chicken in a cunning ploy to make sure Rachel ate, and it worked – no one (apart from vegetarians, obviously) can resist my mum's roast chicken. Every time I have considered vegetarianism, I have just thought of that chicken. And sausages. And rashers. I don't think I would be a good vegetarian at all, really.

TUESDAY ☾

Rachel is meeting Tom tomorrow. Apparently he agrees that they 'have to see each other'. Maybe he has realised that he's made a terrible mistake and will tell her he wants to go out with her again. People sometimes do stupid things and regret it afterwards. I mean, I once told Mrs Harrington that my mother was going to put her in a book. Obviously dumping your girlfriend is not the same as telling a pointless lie to a teacher, but surely it is possible to break up with someone and then regret it afterwards. Maybe he really was having some sort of life crisis about going to college next year, or something, and broke up with her in a moment of madness. I do hope that's what it was. She is still so miserable.

And my parents aren't helping. It was, of course, their musical rehearsal tonight and they almost didn't go because they were worried that if they left the house, and Rachel wasn't under their constant supervision, she would, and I quote, 'sit around moping' instead of doing her homework.

'We do understand how awful it is for you,' said my mother, though I'm not so sure about that. 'But you'll actually feel better if you sit down and do some work.'

'Moping' is possibly my least favourite word ever, because when I was so miserable after Paperboy went to Canada I got accused (by my own best friends, among others) of moping all the time and I hated it. And if anyone actually has an excuse for doing some moping at the moment, it's Rachel. Not that I would call it moping. I would call it 'being heartbroken'.

'She's not moping, Mother!' I said. 'It's not fair to accuse someone of moping when they have just been dumped by their boyfriend who they were going out with for years!'

'Thanks for the reminder, Bex,' said Rachel, but she didn't

sound angry. In fact, for a moment, she almost sounded like her usual annoying sarcastic self.

Anyway, Rachel promised them she would definitely do her homework.

'You can check it and sign it if you want,' she said crossly.

'That's not necessary, love,' said Mum. 'We don't want to nag you.'

Ha! News to me. Nagging both of us is their favourite thing to do after taking part in amateur musicals.

'We just think you need to keep yourself busy,' Mum went on. 'And I know we keep going on about it, but you can't let things slip this year. If you stay on top of schoolwork now, things will be much easier next June.'

'Yes, yes, I know,' said Rachel. 'I'm going off to do it now.'

And she actually did. I thought I might as well show solidarity and do mine too. Also, I wanted to get it over and done with so I could laze around for the rest of the evening and watch whatever I liked on the big sitting-room telly before Mum and Dad came home and took it over with one of the ten million crime dramas they love so much (in fact, crime dramas are possibly their fourth favourite thing after musicals, nagging and going to garden centres).

Rachel eventually came down to join me and admitted that

doing her homework had kept her mind off things.

'It's a sad state of affairs when I have to turn to Leaving Cert Irish to cheer myself up,' she sighed.

And I had to agree. I do wish there was something I could genuinely do to make her feel better. I wish she'd taught me how to make her own famous special hot chocolate so I could make some for her, but she hasn't, so I made her a cup of tea instead. And I made a peppermint one for myself. We both curled up on the couch with our tea and watched a reality show in which people had to make outlandish outfits which was quite fun.

When it was over, I said, 'What do you think will happen with Tom tomorrow?'

'Nothing, probably,' she said. 'He was pretty definite on the phone on Sunday. I just need to see him. I don't think it'll really sink in until I know what it's like to see him when we're not ... when we're not going out anymore.'

She looked really sad. I wondered if she was hoping he'd changed his mind. I know I would be, even if I knew it was stupid. Sometimes you can't help how you feel, even if your brain knows it doesn't make sense. I am hoping he made a mistake myself.

Anyway, that was when our parents came in, singing 'On the Street Where You Live' (even though neither of them are singing that song in the production). I must admit that even though they can be very boring when they start going on about what the director suggested and what song they learned that evening and all that sort of thing, sometimes it does make me a bit nostalgic for my own school musical days. I sort of wish we could do it again this year, but they don't let people who have big exams that year take part.

WEDNESDAY ✿

Poor Rachel. Tom hasn't changed his mind and he doesn't think he's made a mistake. He doesn't want to get back together with her. I think a part of her really did hope this could happen, because she was so upset when she came home. It was like she'd been freshly dumped all over again. She went up to her room, looking like a ghost, and then she was on the phone to Jenny for ages. When the only thing I could hear coming through the door was miserable music I knocked on it.

'I'm not really in the mood for talking' came a leaden voice from within.

'Okay,' I said. I paused. 'I hope it wasn't too awful. Meeting him, I mean.' I didn't even want to say his name, because when you do she looks like she's going to burst into tears.

I could hear Rachel getting off the bed and walking across the room. Then the door opened. Her eyes and nose were really red and it was obvious that she'd been crying.

'It was pretty shit,' she said. She leaned against the door frame and ran her hand through her hair. 'He was really sad and upset and that kind of made it worse. I mean, it shows he really means it and he didn't do it lightly, you know what I mean?'

I did. If Tom is really upset about it, he must have thought about it a lot. But then something struck me.

'Is there a chance he's upset because he realises what a terrible mistake he made?' I said.

Rachel actually laughed, in a reluctant sort of way.

'No, I don't think there is,' she said. 'He's upset because I'm so upset.'

'But that shows he cares about you!' I said.

'He does care about me,' she said. 'But not in the right way. Not anymore.'

And she looked so sad I felt like I wanted to kill Tom.

'I hope he gets run over by a bus,' I said.

She almost laughed again. 'I never thought I'd thank anyone who just wished Tom would be run over by a bus,' she said.

'But ... thanks.'

And then she went back into her room and put the music back on. Music is very good when you're miserable. There's something about hearing someone, someone who might even be dead by now, singing about exactly the same things you're feeling right now that makes you feel like you're not alone. Like someone else gets you, even though you don't know them and you never will.

I wasn't in the mood for miserable music myself this evening, though. I needed some cheering up after talking to Rachel, so I went down to the kitchen and put on one of Mum's Northern Soul compilations and had a bit of a dance. It was very cheering, even when Mum and Dad heard what I was playing and came in and started doing some ridiculous moves. They can actually be quite funny sometimes when they're not being annoying or embarrassing. I almost felt guilty strutting around downstairs when Rachel was up there crying along to the sound of miserable wailing, but her sad music was on so loudly she couldn't have heard us.

THURSDAY ◉

Mrs Harrington started talking to me about her book after class today. Apparently she is sending the first few chapters off to an agent who she hopes will sell the book to a publisher.

'How long do you think I'll have to wait before I hear back?' she asked, and I had to tell her I didn't know. I think she thinks I am some sort of publishing expert because of my mum. It's not like she's looking for favours, or is trying to get my mum to read her book or anything, but she seems to think I know all about it. Which I don't. I mean, if Mum was an engineer she'd hardly ask me about pipes and bridges and things, would she?

Rachel is still spending most of her time in her room. This evening I was putting stuff in the recycling bin in the utility room, and when I opened the bin I saw the giant Valentine's card Tom gave Rachel back in February. It had been torn to pieces. It was weird to see it because I have very strong memories of when she got it – I felt all jealous that day because I was still really sad about Paperboy.

Anyway, I don't blame her for taking out her sadness as rage on Tom's card, but I can't help thinking it's a good sign that she went to the trouble of recycling the card. I mean, if she was totally deranged with grief she wouldn't have thought of sorting her waste in a sensible, environmentally aware fashion, she'd have just chucked the bits of card in the general bin along with Bumpers's old cat litter and stuff.

FRIDAY ☺

Vanessa's ad is going to be on telly on Monday evening. It'll be in the ad break during *Fair City*. We don't always watch *Fair City*, but I will definitely be watching on Monday because – and I'm ashamed to admit it – I do want to see the ad. I know. But I can't help it, even though she was being particularly sickening today. For some reason, she has started talking like a celebrity doing an interview. Maybe she thinks she is about to become really famous and is getting in some practice.

'They say you should never work with children or animals,' she said at lunch, supposedly to Caroline, but so loudly we could all hear it. 'But Handsome Dan was a perfect co-star!'

I don't know whether Handsome Dan is a child or an animal. You'd assume he is an animal with a name like that, but you never know these days. There's a kid in Jessie's little sister's class called Sugar Poppy. Anyway, I wonder what the

Bluebird Bakery would say if they knew Vanessa was giving so many hints about the contents of their top-secret ad? If I were a nasty sort of person, I would tell them and get her fired, but, sadly, I am not.

On the plus side, we're going in to the Knitting Factory tomorrow for our first practice! And Ellie is going in to use the art studio. I wonder will Sam be there? It would be nice to see him. More importantly, I do still have one of his Neil Gaiman books and I have to give it back. I'd contact him online, but I don't want him to read anything into it – me contacting him directly I mean.

LATER

What could he read into it? Why do I care? I'm being ridiculous. If I don't see him tomorrow, I'll send him a message.

SATURDAY ☺

Rachel is feeling even worse today. She and Jenny went out last night and she had a terrible hangover this morning. When

I woke up, I could hear her getting very sick in the bathroom. It was pretty revolting. As she will be eighteen in a few months Mum and Dad don't usually mind Rachel going to over-eighteens places and having the odd drink. Their theory is that if they trust her to behave sensibly, she will then actually behave sensibly because she knows that if she broke their trust and went out and got hammered she would get into loads of trouble and then she wouldn't be allowed out at all.

So far it has worked (with one or two exceptions that Mum and Dad have turned a blind eye to). But they were very annoyed this morning and also a bit upset.

'You can't go drowning your sorrows,' said Dad. 'It's not healthy and it doesn't work.'

Rachel gave a miserable grunt in reply. Mum and Dad lectured her for another while, but eventually they seemed to decide that her puking all day was punishment enough, and she's also not allowed go on any nights out at all for the next month.

I have to say she's not exactly an advertisement for getting off your face. It makes me never want to drink at all (not that I really like the taste of any booze I've tried. Perhaps I am not a natural party animal). Apparently, she and Jenny went to a gig in a place where there was a late bar and were still there drinking shots at two in the morning. It was Jenny's birthday last week and she basically spent all of her birthday money taking Rachel out on the town. Not sure it was worth it today, though.

Anyway, after a while I had to leave her lying on the couch in her pyjamas and go in to our first practice in the new studio space. It was totally brilliant! In fact, I felt a bit guilty being so cheerful when Rachel is still feeling so awful. But it was so good. The practice room we got to use was really nice – even better than the ones in the summer camp – and the drum kit was very cool. It was all red and sparkly (mine is just boring and dark green). And lots of our friends were there. Small Paula was working on something on her own in the recording studio (she is much more technologically advanced than Hey Dollface), and Richard and his band, the Wicked Ways, were in the practice room next to ours.

Even though Cass and I see Richard fairly regularly (and of course Alice sees him all the time), it was cool to see the whole band again. We went in to their room for a bit to hear them play their new song, 'Pterodactyl'. It is all about how sometimes Richard feels like an ancient flying dinosaur looking down on the earth. I had no idea he felt like this, but like all the Wicked Ways songs 'Pterodactyl' is both very melodramatic and strangely impressive. Then they all came in to our practice room to hear our song 'Pistachio' (a very poetic title if I say so myself), which is about looking back at a long ago lost love (Paperboy, of course).

They seemed to like it (or if they didn't, they are very good actors and should have been doing the acting part of the course instead of the rock camp). And the guitarist, Colin, had a useful suggestion about making the intro a bit longer, which we tried after they went back to their room and which worked really well. We are all giving each other feedback like some sort of cool artistic community!

When our studio time was up, we went back to the art studio space part of the venue to meet Ellie, and who should be there but Sam and Lucy! It was very cool to see them. At the end of the summer camp Ellie vowed that she was going to make all her clothes from now on (apart from bras and things) and she has finally finished her first ensemble. It didn't actually look too bad. Well, the skirt was pretty good. It was a plain denim skirt and the only thing wrong with it was a slightly wonky zip, and we wouldn't have noticed if Ellie hadn't pointed it out. She was also wearing a top she'd made herself, but it wasn't quite as successful as the skirt because the shoulders were about twice as wide as the rest of her put together.

'I made a couple of mistakes,' she said. 'The sleeves should be a bit more gathered and a bit less puffy. But I thought I'd just go with it. I think I've made it work.'

I agreed with her because I didn't want to rain on her clothes-making parade, especially as she's just getting started. She needs lots of encouragement and she really can sew, so she'll get better eventually. And, who knows, perhaps she'll start a new trend? After all, huge poofy shoulders were all the rage back in the eighties. Maybe this is the beginning of a revival and we'll all be wearing tops with giant sleeves soon.

Anyway, we were all hanging out chatting for a while, and eventually Cass went off to meet Liz – they were going out to Liz's house. Lucy was going to visit her cousins in Rathmines, so she went to get the bus with them. Alice went off with Richard to have dinner in his house, and Ellie had to go home straight away, so basically I ended up chatting to Sam outside the venue for a while. I told him I still had his book.

'I am going to give it back,' I said. 'In case you thought I'd stolen it.'

'I think I can trust you,' he said. 'Just give it back whenever you like. You're going to be here fairly regularly, aren't you?'

'Yeah, I hope so,' I said. 'Every week, I think.'

'Me too,' he said. 'This place is great, isn't it?'

And we talked about the Knitting Factory for a bit. We both agree that it makes a big difference when you have somewhere special to go and do something creative (making comics for him, band practice for me). Sam wants to go to art college and study illustration eventually.

'I think my actual dream job would be sitting in a nice big studio and just drawing all day,' he said. 'What about you?'

'Hmm,' I said. 'I think I'd like to spend half my time drumming and half my time writing stuff.'

'Sounds doable,' said Sam. I wonder has he grown since the summer? He looks taller. 'I mean,' he went on, 'it's probably more doable than my mate Daire's dream of being a professional surfer.'

'Is he not a good surfer?' I said.

'Well, he's only done it once, in Donegal,' said Sam. 'So I'm kind of surprised he's so convinced he could do it for a living. But he's quite a good skateboarder, and he claims they use the same skills. I'm not sure how, though, apart from the whole "standing on a bit of board" aspect.'

We just stood there chatting about rubbish for a while. He is very easy to talk to. But eventually my phone beeped – just a text from Rachel asking me to get some milk on my way home – and I realised we'd been talking for over half an hour.

'God, is it that late?' said Sam, when I mentioned the time. 'I'm meant to be going out for dinner for my dad's birthday this evening. I'd better get home and change.'

'Is it a fancy dinner?' I said.

'Ah, not really,' said Sam. 'But my mum will kill me if I turn up covered in ink yet again.' He gestured to his t-shirt, which had a splash of blue ink on it. 'It should be good fun, really. They do really good fancy burgers in the restaurant, and my aunt and uncle and my cousin Jim are coming too – they're always a good laugh.'

John Kowalski used to act like having to go out for a family dinner was the worst thing in the world. It's quite refreshing to see some boys don't think having to eat nice food is a terrible torture. Anyway, we walked out to the bus stops together (his is just down the road from mine) and said we'd probably see each other next week. He didn't mention Gemma and I didn't really want to ask. I wouldn't want him to get the wrong idea and think I cared who he went out with. Or didn't. Whatever the case may be.

When I got home my parents were out (at the garden centre yet again – what can they be buying there? It's not like we have spacious grounds to put loads of plants and things in. Our garden is only about ten metres long). Rachel was slumped on the couch watching one of the music channels and looking pretty miserable (which is kind of her default state at the moment. In fact, unless I actually say otherwise, you should probably assume that she looks miserable all the time).

'Are you okay?' I said.

'This time last week Tom was telling me it was all over,' she said. 'And now this is my life. Sitting on the couch watching telly on a Saturday night. Well, evening.'

Sitting on the couch watching telly on a Saturday night has basically been my life for ages and it's not that bad, but she was so miserable I couldn't feel too insulted. In fact, she looked so sorry for herself I went all the way to the shops and got her a can of Coke. Sometimes I think I am more like a saint than a sister.

SUNDAY ☼

I decided I would have to try cheering Rachel up today. She spent all morning lying on the couch reading Mum's old poetry books from college. It was a piteous sight. She can't go on like this forever, but she hasn't shown any signs of doing anything else so I knew I had to do something to help her along the way. But what? If I had loads of money, I could, like, take her out and have lots of exciting adventures and buy her loads of cool stuff, but sadly all I had in my purse today was a five euro note and that wouldn't go far. I couldn't even take her to the cinema with it, and my parents had gone to visit my annoying aunt (luckily they hadn't insisted on taking us with them) so I couldn't get any money out of them.

Anyway, out of desperation, I decided to take Rachel for a walk. After all, fresh air is meant to be good for you, isn't it? Of course, it wasn't easy to persuade her.

'I don't want to go for a walk!' she said.

'It'll be nice!' I said. 'The autumn leaves! The beauties of nature!'

'What beauties of nature?' she said. 'There isn't any nature round here.'

She had a point. The nearest park just looks like a big flat playing field. But then I thought of something.

'The teacher-training college!' I said. 'That's got lots of nature – well, it's got trees and squirrels and things – and it's only round the corner.'

'I am not getting off this nice cosy couch to go out and walk around the grounds of a bloody teacher-training col-lege,' said Rachel.

'But it will stop you thinking about Tom,' I said. 'I mean,

you don't want him to think that you're just ... ' I nearly said 'moping' for a second, but then I stopped myself. 'That you're just staying at home all the time?'

I didn't remind her that she had definitely not stayed at home on Friday night. Anyway, for some reason it worked.

'Oh God, I'll come for a stupid walk if it'll shut you up,' she said.

A few minutes later, we were walking down to the teacher-training college. I'm not sure if you're actually allowed to walk around the grounds if you're not a student there, but they never seem to care. Cass and I have been known to walk around there discussing the important things in life, like whether Paperboy was ever going to come back from Canada, the latest developments in *Laurel Canyon* and what we'd call our autobiographies if we wrote them (Cass's would be called *From School to Stage: The Cass McDermott Story*. Mine would be called *Sticks and Stones*, which is a witty reference to my drum sticks. The stones bit doesn't really mean anything. I just put it in because it's the only phrase I could think of that has sticks in it).

It was actually rather nice just strolling down the hill because the weather was almost summery today.

'See!' I said to Rachel. 'Look how warm and sunny it is!

You'd have missed this niceness if you were stuck indoors.'

'Shut up or I'm turning around and going home,' said Rachel, so I stopped pointing out how pleasant it was.

A few minutes later, we walked through the gates of the college (which have some excellent dragons on them that are over two hundred years old). There were flowers and nice big old trees everywhere and I actually felt more relaxed myself. I looked over at Rachel and saw she looked slightly less grumpy too. At least she didn't have a hangover today, so that was another plus.

'So we're here,' she said. 'Trespassing. Where do we go now?'

'Cass and I usually do a circuit of the grounds,' I said. 'What do you think?'

'Oh, why not?' said Rachel, not exactly enthusiastically. So off we went. Neither of us said anything for a while, but it wasn't a bad sort of silence. It was all very peaceful. A squirrel paused while running between two trees and stared at us in a defiant sort of way. It felt like being in the countryside.

'Vanessa's ad is going to be on telly tomorrow,' I said at last.

'God, really?' said Rachel. She has seen Vanessa in action before and knows how annoying she is. 'That's all I need. I'm not sure I'll be able to take that in my current emotional state.'

It was only the second time since the break-up that I've

heard her make a sort of joke about it. I took this as a good sign.

'She sings a song in it and everything,' I said. 'She says they might release it as a single!'

Rachel made a snorting sound that was almost – but not quite – a laugh.

'I am fairly sure that is not going to happen,' she said.

'I wouldn't be so sure,' I said. 'Cass said the other day that we should never underestimate Vanessa and she's been proved right. She did get this ad, after all.'

'Well, if she ends up in the charts, then I'll know the world really doesn't make any sense anymore,' said Rachel. She kicked some fallen leaves. It was obvious that she was thinking about Tom again, which was not part of my cheering up plan. So I told her what Mum had said about the new Ruthie O'Reilly book.

'She swears she didn't put anything about us in the book this time,' I said.

'She'd better not have,' said Rachel. 'I still can't believe she put in that story about Jenny and the ... well, never mind.'

'You never did tell me what story she stole!' I said. 'Go on!'

'I can't,' said Rachel, but she was smiling. 'It's Jenny's story, not mine. And I'm still a loyal friend. You wouldn't tell me about Cass or Alice, would you?'

'I suppose not,' I said. 'Anyway, the book's not going to be out for a while, so we have plenty of time to prepare. Unlike last time.'

'Yeah, I think our parents have given us more than enough surprises over the last year,' said Rachel. 'What with ridiculous books and Dad being a dancing legend.'

'I still find that kind of hard to believe,' I said. 'I mean, I almost think I dreamed it. If you and my friends hadn't been there to witness it, I'd really think I had. I wonder what he's doing to liven up Henry Higgins.'

'God, yeah,' said Rachel. 'I'd forgotten about that. What can he be doing? High-kicking across the stage while other people are singing, probably.'

'He wouldn't do that!' I said, but as soon as the words were out of my mouth I realised they weren't true. There is a chance he could do that. He's dancing mad. 'Oh God, he probably would,' I said.

At this stage, we had done a circuit of the training college grounds so we wandered out of the gates and headed home-wards. I didn't want to mention You-Know-Who, especially as we'd managed to talk about other things for the entire walk, but, as we walked up Glandore Road, I realised Rachel had been thinking about him anyway because she suddenly said, 'He'd have told me if there was somebody else, wouldn't he?'

I didn't bother pretending that I didn't know who 'he' was.

'Yeah, I suppose so,' I said, even though I wasn't actually sure. Then I thought of something. 'I mean, when would he have had a chance to meet someone else? You saw him all the time until ... well, you know.'

I'm afraid that might have sounded like I was reminding her that they weren't seeing each other at all now, but she didn't seem to think about that.

'Yeah, you're right,' she said. She sighed. 'God, I'm boring myself talking about it now.'

'Did, um, did the walk distract you a bit?' I said. We had just reached the top of our road.

Rachel looked quite surprised.

'Yeah, actually,' she said. 'I mean, sort of. Ah, it got me out of the house. Thanks, Bex.'

'It's all right,' I said. And then we were home and, to be honest, for once I was kind of relieved that our parents were there, being noisy and telling us to go and do some homework, because I am still not used to Rachel looking to me for romantic advice and guidance. It is meant to be the other way round. In fact, I almost miss the times when she was being patronising and annoying and we kept insulting each other. Her being so miserable makes me feel weird as well as sad.

MONDAY ☀

Oh.

My.

God.

I have seen Vanessa's ad. I suspect everyone I know has seen Vanessa's ad. And I think it might be the worst thing I've seen on television EVER. You might think it'd be hard to tell whether the ad is just bad because of Vanessa or whether it would be terrible anyway, but Rachel and I both agree that it would be terrible even if someone else was in it.

Here's what happened. Rachel and I were in the sitting room watching *Fair City* and when the ad break started I was surprised at how nervous/excited I felt. After all, we'd been listening to Vanessa talk about this ad for weeks and now I was going to actually see it. Though now I wish I hadn't. Anyway, first of all there was an ad for a phone company and the next thing I knew the screen was full of Vanessa's face in black and white! A sort of jaunty bassline played as she pretended to be asleep in a bedroom full of vintage trinkets and posters – there was a 'Keep Calm and Carry On' poster and another one with a big castle symbol and the words 'Dublin's Great in '88', which Mum said was the slogan when Dublin was supposedly a thousand years old back in 1988.

Then Vanessa stretched and opened her eyes and everything turned into colour. She was wearing a genuinely cool pair of navy polka dot pyjamas. She looked at the camera, smiled, then reached out of bed, picked up a bright pink ukulele and started to play chords on it. I am pretty sure that if Vanessa could actually play a musical instrument we would have heard all about it during the summer camp, so I can only assume she was miming. Anyway, that was all bad enough, but then, still looking straight into the camera, Vanessa said, 'Hi. I'm Kookie. And I've got a message for everyone out there who feels a little bit, well, quirky. Like me!' Even though she was meant to have just woken up, she was wearing perfect make-up.

And then she began to sing the most annoying song I've ever heard in my life.

> *Everyone's a little bit kooky*
> *Everybody in their own way*
> *So what's the point in being so snooty?*

Have yourself a kooky little day!

I think my mouth might have dropped open with horror.

'Whoah,' said Rachel.

Then the ad cut to Vanessa dressed in a really cute little dress with a white collar. Except it didn't matter how nice the dress was because she was prancing around still pretending (probably) to play the ukulele and smiling in a horrible sickly way.

Some people think I'm totally crazy
Because I always like to sing and play.
But I just want to romp in the daisies
Have yourself a kooky little day!

While she was singing, she skipped out the front door, accompanied by a very, very cute pug with a lovely smiley face. He must be Handsome Dan! Poor little thing, how unfair that he has to share his moment of stardom with someone as awful as Vanessa. The ad cut to her riding a really cool 1950s-style American bike down a street of redbrick houses. Handsome Dan was sitting in the basket in a special harness which didn't look very safe to me, but he looked cheerful enough even though Vanessa was still singing.

Then we saw her arrive at a cute little shop that said Bluebird Bakery over the door. She and Handsome Dan strolled in and she went up to the counter, where there was a big display of Bluebird Bakery Yummy Scrummy Cookies, complete with an old-fashioned china plate piled high with cookies. Vanessa picked one up, took a quick bite and sort of wrinkled her nose with pleasure. It was a sickening sight. Then she looked at the camera again and said: 'And the perfect treat on a kooky little day – or any day – is a Bluebird Bakery Yummy Scrummy Cookie!'

Then she sang the last verse of her dreadful ditty.

> *I'm always going to do my own thing*
> *I don't care what other people say*
> *So let your life go with a swing*
> *Have yourself a kooky little day!*

'Some people might think I'm, well, a little bit strange,' said Vanessa. And then she winked at the camera as the words 'Bluebird Bakery Yummy Scrummy Cookies' appeared on the screen. 'But that's the way the cookie crumbles!'

And that was it.

It was even worse than I could have imagined. Not only was Vanessa incredibly irritating in it, but it took loads of things that would be very nice on their own – like miniature musical instruments and pugs and old bikes – and put them all together and made them look all affected and cutesy and silly. And as for the song – well, words almost fail me, but not quite. I have never heard anything more annoying in my life, and not just because they rhymed 'kooky' with 'snooty'. Those words don't rhyme! Don't they have a rhyming dictionary? There are loads of words that actually rhyme with 'kooky'! Like 'spooky'! And 'fluky'! That line could have been something like 'So don't be afraid that I'm spooky', or something. Not that that's particularly good, but then, it's a terrible song to begin with.

And then there was that even worse catchphrase at the end. That's the way the cookie crumbles indeed! Handsome Dan was the best thing by far in the whole ad. I wish the entire thing was just him going around by himself being awesome and puglike. That would make me want to buy biscuits. He could have carried the cookies around his neck in a little basket or something. I just feel sorry for him having to work with Vanessa for an entire weekend. I know he is merely a dog, but they do say animals are very sensitive when it comes to people's personalities, so he must have known how awful she is.

On the plus side, this evening was the first time I've seen Rachel laugh properly since the dumping. When Vanessa cycled off, with Handsome Dan in the basket, singing about having a kooky little day, she let out a proper big honk of laughter.

'This is amazing,' she said.

Then I made her shut up because for some weird reason I didn't want to miss the rest of the awful song. I must be a masochist.

As soon as it was over, my phone beeped. It was a text from Cass and simply read, 'Won't be in school tomorrow cos I have been struck blind and deaf by that ad.'

I rang her because this was another issue that needed to be discussed in person. She didn't even say hello when answering the phone. She just said, 'It was worse than I thought.'

'I know,' I said. 'Apart from Handsome Dan.'

'Oh yes, I liked him,' said Cass. 'But otherwise I am trying to think how it could have been more annoying and I actually don't think it could.'

'She's going to be worse than ever now,' I said. And we both sighed because we know this is true. She was pretty bad at school today and that was before the ad had even aired. She accosted me when I was going to the loo at lunchtime.

'So, Rebecca,' she said. 'Is your mother still doing that whole writing for teenagers thing?'

'Um, yes, unfortunately,' I said, wondering what was going to come next. The last time Vanessa showed any interest in my mother was when she decided Mum's supposed fame would help her get on a reality TV show. 'The next one's coming out before Christmas.'

'Great,' said Vanessa. 'Are there any plans for a TV series?'

'What?' I said. 'No! Not as far as I know.'

'Well, if there is,' said Vanessa, 'just let her know I might be available. Of course, it depends how the Kookie campaign develops. I might be too busy. But I'm sure she'd want her daughter's friend to play a lead role.'

'I don't think she'd have any say in the matter,' I said. I didn't bother pointing out that Vanessa has only ever seen herself as my friend when she thought she could get something from me.

'Just let her know I'm interested,' said Vanessa, ignoring what I'd just said (as usual). And she strolled off.

The thing is, and I hate to say it, but I actually think she would be pretty good at playing the awful Ruthie O'Reilly. She's certainly obnoxious enough.

Anyway, now I am faced with the prospect of seeing that ad every time I turn on my telly. What a thought. Still, it was good to see Rachel laughing like a loon again, even though she does have quite a honking laugh (she inherited it from Dad. Mum still laughs like a horse. I hope I haven't inherited either of their weird animal-like laughs. I don't think I have, but you never know. Maybe I am so used to it I can't tell that I sound like some weird goose-horse hybrid).

Rachel said she hadn't thought it was possible for Vanessa to be so sweet and sugary. 'I kept expecting her to say that she believed in fairies and that the stars were God's daisy chain or something,' she said. The ad had definitely cheered her up. She looked positively happy. So maybe Vanessa can be a force for good after all.

TUESDAY ☾

I don't understand the world anymore. Nothing makes sense. Today was even worse than I feared. Unsurprisingly, everyone at school saw the ad last night. But very surprisingly, everyone at school seems to love it! Girls from other classes kept sticking their heads into our form room at lunch, trying to catch a glimpse of Vanessa. They were even following her around as she went from class to class. I swear to God, some of them were even asking for her autograph. And she, of course, was in her element.

'Form an orderly queue, girls,' she commanded as a bunch of first years held out pieces of paper.

'They're too young to know any better,' said Alice.

'I don't know,' said Cass. 'When we were their age, we certainly wouldn't have wanted to get Vanessa's autograph.'

We mightn't have had a choice. She was actually offering to sign people's copies and folders during the mid-morning break. I half expected her to start grabbing them out of our hands and scrawling all over them.

'I told you I wouldn't forget you all when my ad came out,' she assured us. 'And I won't!'

If only she would. The thing about Vanessa is that you simply can't ignore her because she won't let you, so she is a constant source of annoyance. Of course, none of us (not even Caroline and Karen) took her up on her autograph offer, but she didn't care. At one stage, in our form room during lunch break, when the flood of girls from other classes had died down, she turned to me and said, 'So, what did you think of the ad?'

I said the only polite thing I could think of.

'Um, it was very colourful,' I said. 'I liked Handsome Dan.'

'Oh yeah,' said Vanessa. 'He was a pro. I actually asked his owner about buying him. I thought it would be good for the brand if we were seen walking around together in public.'

What a terrible fate for poor Handsome Dan! Imagine being bought by Vanessa purely as a marketing tool and forced to parade through the streets with her. Luckily, his owner immediately said no. Apparently, she runs a performing-animal agency called The Li'l Tykes and has two other dogs of her own which also appear in ads. What a brilliant job that must be – just hanging around with nice, cheerful dogs all day and teaching them how to ride in bike baskets (because putting a dog in a bike basket should only be done under expert supervision). Although, on the downside, you'd have to hang around with people like Vanessa too. Still, swings and roundabouts, as my annoying aunt likes to say.

'I didn't realise you could play the ukulele, Vanessa,' said Alice politely.

Vanessa looked at her in a very patronising way.

'I can't,' she said. 'I was doing a little thing I like to call … acting.'

And because Alice has much better manners than I do, she just said, 'Oh. Well, it looked very realistic.'

'Yeah, I know,' said Vanessa, and before any of us could say anything else she turned back towards her fan club (aka Karen and Caroline. Alison was there too, but she looked very bored). Karen started telling them how Bernard the Fairytale Prince went over to her house last night so they could watch the ad together.

'You're an inspiration to us all,' said Karen to Vanessa. 'Bernard and I are going to start looking out for auditions ourselves.'

Vanessa looked a bit taken aback for a moment. Clearly she didn't like the idea of someone else, especially her devoted pal, stealing her thunder. But then she seemed to decide that being copied was another form of flattery, as well as an opportunity to show off even more.

'Good idea,' she said. 'I'll be able to give you plenty of tips.'

The thing is, she probably could. She does seem to know what she's doing. Whatever I might think about her, she clearly has the x-factor, or whatever factor you need to do well in advertising. And if our school is anything to go by, people really do seem to love the ad. I was in the loo between classes this afternoon and I overheard some second years talking about it.

'It's just so cute!' said one of them.

'And I love the song,' said the other. 'Did you see the posters? There's one on the bus stop on Drumcondra Road. As soon as I saw it this morning, the song got stuck in my head again.'

I had forgotten about the posters. I can only imagine what they're like. I'd like to hope they just show Handsome Dan and some biscuits, but I'm pretty sure they're all about Vanessa. She seems to be everywhere. It's funny (and not in a funny ha-ha way), she's been telling herself that she's a celebrity for years and now she actually is one. I'm not sure that Rachel laughing again is worth it if it's given Vanessa an actual legitimate reason to believe she's a superstar.

Anyway, I didn't see the ad again today because I didn't watch much telly tonight, even though Mum and Dad were out at their rehearsal so Rachel and I could have had the sitting-room telly to ourselves. Instead, I put a playlist of some of my favourite songs on the stereo and played along on my snare drum. It's good practice, even though we don't want to do cover versions with Hey Dollface. I also played the recording of our own song 'The Real Me' that we made during the summer camp. It still sounds pretty good, if I say so myself. I hope we'll get to try recording more stuff soon at the Knitting Factory.

Anyway, I do appreciate being able to play the drum(s) at home more than ever now since I realised I might have to give them back. I suppose I was making quite a lot of noise, but for once Rachel didn't mind because she was on the phone to Jenny for hours on end, talking very intensely about Tom. Well, I presume it was about Tom. Every time I went upstairs to go to the loo or get something from my room, I could hear Rachel through the door saying things like 'I just don't understand why he could change his mind about me'. Later, I heard her say something like, 'Oh, I dunno, Jen. I just miss him.'

That was when I felt really bad for her. I know I really, really missed Paperboy when he flew off to Canada, but apart from the fact I knew he hadn't chosen to leave me, I hadn't actually been going out with him for very long. Not that that meant I wasn't really, really sad, or that my sadness wasn't serious, but he hadn't had time to become, like, an integral part of my life. Whereas Rachel and Tom saw each other all the time for years, so he's left a big hole in her life.

She just needs something to fill it up. Not another boy (yet). But something else. I mean, if I've learned anything this year, apart from lots of scary facts about climate change courtesy of Miss Kelly, it's that going out with someone is just, like, a bonus. There was a stage, in the summer, when I was kind of depressed that all my best friends were going out with people and I wasn't, and I didn't even fancy anyone. But I had a really good chat with Daisy which basically made me realise that if everything else in my life is actually good and fun (more or less), then I should enjoy it and stop worrying that I will never love anyone ever again. I suppose that if I still haven't met anyone I like by the time I'm, I dunno, thirty or something I might start to worry. But, in the meantime, I feel more or less okay. And so will Rachel. She just doesn't know it yet.

I must try and think of fun things for her to do to stop – I almost said moping there. I meant being miserable. I almost wish she was into amateur dramatics (not that it would help if she was, I suppose, because it's her Leaving Cert year and she wouldn't have time to do them) because my parents certainly seem to get a lot of fun from their production of *My Fair Lady*. Too much fun, if you ask me. They were singing as usual when they came home tonight, or at least Dad was.

'How did your rehearsal go?' I asked.

'Very well,' said Dad, looking pleased with himself. 'I really think my interpretation of Henry Higgins is going to be pretty interesting.'

'What does the director think?' I said.

'She likes it!' said Dad. 'It's her first time directing, remember, so I think she welcomes creative input. Doesn't she, Rosie?'

'Um, yes,' said Mum. 'She does. I'm not sure Dearbhla would have been so ... open-minded.'

Dearbhla was the old director.

'What sort of things are you doing?' I asked Dad.

'Oh, you know,' said Dad. 'A dance step here, some jazz hands there. Whatever feels natural.'

'Ah,' I said. 'I see.'

When he'd gone upstairs to put away his tap shoes, I went over to Mum.

'Mum,' I said. 'You know the way Dad's jazzing up Henry Higgins.'

'Yes?' said Mum, in a rather wary voice.

'He's not ... well, he's not going too far, is he?' I said.

There was a pause.

'I wouldn't say that,' she said. 'He's got great stage presence, as you know.'

I nodded.

'But yes, he's taken a very ... well, it's not how Henry Higgins is normally played. He's usually shown as a sort of reserved, haughty character. Now he's a bit more, well ... vibrant.'

'Vibrant,' I said. 'Wow.' I could well imagine how vibrant he was.

'But the director doesn't seem to mind it!' said Mum, brightly. 'So I'm sure it'll all work out! Now I'd better put away my own dance shoes.' And she basically ran out of the room so she didn't have to say anything else about it.

I am pretty sure this means that Dad has let his Beadle triumph go to his head and is prancing all over the place like a loon. I just hope he doesn't push it with the new director. She might decide he's jazzed up Henry Higgins a bit too much and take the part away from him! And surely having a lead part, even if it doesn't involve loads of jazz hands, is better than no part at all?

WEDNESDAY ❀

Even our teachers are talking about Vanessa's ad. It has caused a sensation. Mrs Harrington told her it was 'the cutest little thing she'd ever seen' yesterday, which I suppose is what I'd expect from someone whose taste is so bad she thinks my mother's books are the greatest works of literature ever written.

More surprisingly, Miss Kelly brought it up in geography today. I didn't think Miss Kelly would approve of any ads, given how much energy they cost to make and how opposed she is to consumerism in general, but she clearly doesn't have a problem with this one.

'I like your ad, Miss Finn,' she said. 'Good to see someone using a bicycle on screen! And Bluebird Bakery are committed to ethical trading and sustainable business. They use Irish suppliers whenever possible.'

I don't know why she was praising Vanessa for this. It's not like she makes the biscuits herself. But Vanessa took the praise as her due.

'I'm proud to be a Bluebird Bakery spokeswoman,' she said, in a ridiculously grown-up way.

'And that's a very catchy song, too!' said Miss Kelly.

For a moment, I was afraid she was going to start singing it, but luckily she just moved on and started talking about how if flooding patterns continue all of Dublin will be under water in a few years. Which was actually more cheering than hearing about Vanessa's ad. At least if we're all under water, we won't have to watch her poncing around on that bike.

Miss Kelly was right, though, it is a very catchy song, even though it's incredibly annoying and doesn't rhyme properly. I found myself singing it this evening when I was loading the dishwasher. As soon as I realised what I was doing, I felt ashamed of myself, but I was still humming the song an hour later. That's all I need, Vanessa's ad stuck in my head! It's bad enough having to watch it when it airs, which it did twice this evening. Mum and Dad saw it too.

'She was in your production of *Mary Poppins*, wasn't she?' said Dad. 'She's very ... cheerful.'

'It's just an act,' I said grumpily. 'She's a stuck-up egomaniac in real life.'

'The dog's very cute,' said Mum. 'And the production design is great. And she can sing very well!'

'She wants to play Ruthie if they make a film or a TV series from your book,' I told her.

Mum looked a bit taken aback. 'Really?' she said. 'I didn't imagine Ruthie being quite so ... in your face.'

'I did,' I said, because Ruthie certainly felt just as annoying as Vanessa to me.

Mum seemed quite insulted by the thought that Vanessa could be a perfect Ruthie, but I'm afraid it serves her right for embarrassing me by creating such an irritating character.

Also, Sorcha Mulligan is up to her old tricks again. I was doing my homework just now and she and one of her friends were both standing at the window, staring at me in a scary way. So she seems to have given up on the dancing. I'd be relieved, except this is actually more unsettling. Anyway, I just ignored her, but I couldn't help looking up every so often and I swear, they were always in the same place. It can't be normal for a kid to do this, can it? Oh well, it could be worse, I suppose. She could be skipping around pretending to play the ukulele.

LATER

Oh God, I hope I haven't tempted fate just by writing that. The last thing I need is to look up and see the Mulligan kid playing a ukulele, or even just waving one at me. I just hope she doesn't see Vanessa's ad and get notions.

THURSDAY ◎

I wish I could just stay away from school until all the fuss over Vanessa has died down. I got a lift to school today because Mum had to go into town and she ended up dropping me off at a bus stop that had a giant poster of Vanessa on it. She stood there smirking with a ukulele in one hand and a cookie in the other, and the words 'Have Yourself a Kooky Little Day' were emblazoned above her head in quite cool pink letters. Handsome Dan was on the poster too, but he was at Vanessa's feet so you barely noticed him.

And Vanessa was just as bad in real life today too. She brought in her iPad purely so she could show us all the bit of the Bluebird Bakery website devoted to 'Kookie'.

'I could have just shown you on my phone, of course,' she said. 'But you need a larger screen to get the full effect.'

She basically marched around the class shoving her stupid posh 3G iPad in people's faces. I suppose she knew it's the only way we'd ever see the website – I certainly wasn't going to look it up at home. Anyway, unsurprisingly, the website was terrible. As soon as you opened the page, an animated Vanessa cycled across it and winked out at you, which would have been bad enough on its own. Then the words 'Have Yourself a Kooky Little Day!' appeared over her head in the same cute retro lettering as the poster, along with a pack of Bluebird Bakery Yummy Scrummy Cookies. Several links popped up on one side of the page. The top one had a picture of Vanessa's face with the words 'All about Kookie!'

I can't imagine anyone would want to know all about Kookie, or indeed anything about Kookie, but I didn't have any choice in the matter because Vanessa clicked on the image and, a moment later, we were looking at yet another picture of her smirking features. Obviously, I wouldn't have bothered reading what was written underneath, but unfortunately Vanessa immediately began reading it all out loud.

'Meet Kookie!' she began. 'She's not like everyone else. But then, neither are you!'

Cass and I looked at each other and rolled our eyes.

'Kookie likes to dance her way through life,' Vanessa read on. 'She's always looking for fun, quirky things to do by herself, with her friends or with her cheeky pet pug, Handsome Dan.'

It's good to know that Handsome Dan is being credited by name, I suppose.

'She loves old French films, 1980s pop music and playing her hot pink ukulele,' Vanessa continued. 'That's how kooky she is! But there's one thing Kookie has in common with everyone else – she loves Yummy Scrummy Cookies.' Vanessa looked at us as if she expected us to applaud. 'That's it.'

'Wow,' said Alice, polite as ever. I don't know how she does it. 'Very cool.'

Actually, I think those words crossed over from 'politeness' to 'barefaced lie'. But they seemed to satisfy Vanessa, and she went off to show the site to some other unfortunates.

You know, sometimes I wonder what would happen if we all started being as rude and arrogant to Vanessa as she is to all of us. Maybe it would show her the error of her ways, but I have a feeling she wouldn't even notice.

Also, I think it's very unfair that she has an iPad at all. There is no chance of my parents splashing out so much money on one for me. My mum has one but she barely lets me use it in case I 'drop it and break it'. As if I would! I only dropped it once and it fell on the sofa so it was fine. Not that she even knows about that. Anyway, I would love a tablet, but considering my parents will only let me have a crappy phone that is like something out of the olden days and can barely go online, I think I will be waiting a long time until I get one. Every time I tell my parents how unfair this is, they just laugh and tell me they didn't have mobiles at all until they were in their mid-thirties.

'And we grew up perfectly well,' says Dad, which is a matter for debate if you ask me.

Anyway, as if all that wasn't bad enough, I think I am getting a spot. It hasn't emerged yet, but I can feel it lurking under the surface. I suppose I am lucky because I don't get spots that often (presumably because nature realised having hair that often looks like a bushy mop is more than enough trauma for one girl), but when I do they are awful. This one is on my chin and I just know that it's going to get bigger and redder for ages until my whole chin looks like Rudolph the Reindeer's nose. I asked my mum this morning when you finally stop getting spots and she said, 'Oh, I don't know, I still get the odd spot now.' And she is forty-eight! It hardly seems fair that I have over twenty more years of lurkers ahead of me.

Anyway, I am going to go and watch some telly now because my parents are out at an extra rehearsal. It seems they might have more than one rehearsal a week from now on as the self-defence class that used to be in the hall on Thursday nights has had to move to a bigger venue, so the musical society are taking advantage of the free space. Before they went, Dad said the cast were 'coming along in leaps and bounds'. I hope he didn't mean literally. I can imagine him leaping and bounding all over the place only too well.

FRIDAY ⌣

Lurking spot is still getting bigger, ready to emerge in all its disgusting glory. It looks redder than ever today. I thought about covering it up with make-up, but when I tried, it looked kind of flaky which was worse than just being red, so I washed it all off. It was like the make-up drew even more attention to my hideous blemish. I wondered if I could get away with hiding it from the world by covering my face with my hands a lot, but I remembered Mum saying before that you should try and avoid touching spots with your hands because you can spread bacteria from your hands to your face. I am pretty sure my hands are nice and clean – I mean, I wash them fairly regularly – but I'm not taking any chances. One spot is bad enough.

So I just had to go in to school and hope that my red, swollen chin didn't look quite as hideous as I thought. Cass and Alice assured me it didn't.

'You can barely see it,' said Cass.

'I wouldn't even have noticed it if you hadn't pointed it out!' said Alice.

I know they were lying, but they meant well. Unlike Vanessa. I ended up queuing in the loo next to her at lunchtime and she suddenly stared at me and said, in her usual abrupt and rude fashion, 'What's that on your chin?'

I glared at her as ferociously as I could.

'A spot,' I said.

'Wow,' said Vanessa. 'I thought you had some, like, skin disease. I was worrying it was contagious.'

'Well, it's not,' I said. 'It's just a totally normal spot.'

'That's a relief,' said Vanessa. 'I've got to do lots of promotional events for Bluebird Bakery this weekend. I wouldn't want to be covered in, like, boils or whatever.'

Boils! I know I am paranoid about this spot, and I know it's not that bad, is it? Surely it is just a normal pimple. A lurking spot, but a normal spot nevertheless. Anyway, I wish I'd actually told Vanessa it was a hideous contagious skin disease just to freak her out, but it's too late now.

LATER

I went to Mum and asked her if she thought I should go to the doctor about the spot. She laughed in her usual callous fashion and said, 'No, Bex, I don't. It's just a normal spot. And it's not that bad!'

'Well, Vanessa Finn thought it was a boil,' I said.

Mum looked very cross when I said this.

'Well, it was very silly and rude of her to say that to you,' she said.

Which I knew already, but it was quite nice to hear Mum say it.

Band practice in the Knitting Factory tomorrow. Hopefully my spot will have disappeared by then. Or if that's too much to hope for, maybe it will have just gone down a bit. Maybe it will never burst forth at all and just sink back down again? I can but hope.

SATURDAY ☺

So … something a bit weird happened today. Not huge and weird like Vanessa being famous, and not sad and weird like Tom dumping Rachel. Just …

Oh, I might as well just say it. I think I like Sam. In fact, I might have liked Sam for a while. And I mean, I like-like him. Not just in a cool-boy-I'm-friends-with way. In a fancying way. But I don't think he likes me back. In that way. At least, I'm not sure. Oh God, it's so weird! But I have to admit, it's been sort of sneaking up on me for ages.

It happened like this. We had booked a practice room at the Knitting Factory for twelve o'clock, and we had decided that we'd get sandwiches and meet Ellie in the arts space afterwards for a sort of indoor picnic lunch thing. The practice was pretty good, although we did almost have an argument over whether to change the ending of 'Pistachio' or not. We didn't come to a fixed conclusion in the end because Alice and I thought it should just end suddenly after the last chorus and Cass thought we should repeat the chorus about a million times until our listeners fell asleep (she didn't say that last bit, but that's what would happen if she had her way). Clearly she was wrong, but neither of us would back down. Still, we're having a workshop with our old band mentor Kitty next week (hurrah!), so maybe she can decide what sounds best.

Anyway, we agreed to disagree for the moment and went off to Centra to get our sandwiches. They were a bit manky, but sadly manky Centra sandwiches are all us youthful musicians can afford. I must admit that, despite my hideous spot not having gone away, I was sort of hoping Sam would be there when we went back to the Knitting Factory, and my hopes were fulfilled because when we went into the big art studio there he was, sitting on a drawing table talking to Ellie, Lucy and a boy we hadn't met before, who turned out to be called Senan. Sam and Lucy seemed pleased to see us (Senan seemed happy enough, but I presume he wasn't hugely excited to see us, considering he'd never set eyes on us before that moment).

They had just done a class with a visiting artist and were all excited about it. Her name is Maria Hanff and she usually makes giant sculptures out of trowels and old flower pots (maybe she goes to the same garden centre as my parents?), but apparently she can draw as well so she was teaching them about life drawing. This is when some poor person sits there without moving for hours on end while a bunch of people draw them. Sometimes the person is in the nude, so the artists learn how to draw the human body in all its glory, but of course this does not happen in an art class for teenagers who are in secondary school, so they all just drew a fully clothed man who Maria Hanff had dragged in from the Knitting Factory offices.

Ellie, Lucy, Sam and Senan's pictures were pretty good, even though the Knitting Factory office man looked very bored, as most people would if they had to sit there for ages doing nothing while several strangers stared at them. Alice said she thought it might be quite peaceful and like meditating, but I tried meditating once after reading a book belonging to my Mum (well, I read the back of the book and the introduction), and it was pretty boring. I only lasted about two minutes. Alice says if I'd read the rest of the book, I might have learned how to do it properly, which is fair enough.

Anyway. We all sat there looking at the pictures and eating sandwiches and chatting for a while. It was so relaxed and fun that, after a while, I forgot to be self-conscious about my stupid giant spot. In fact, I forgot all about it. All the art people are into different sorts of art: Lucy and Sam like comics, Ellie likes designing and making clothes, and Senan wants to make giant oil paintings (which is why, as he said, it's so useful having access to the studio. It's not easy to do giant oil paintings in a semi-detached house in Killester). But they all agreed it was really useful learning how to draw actual people properly.

'I'm still not very good at doing hands, though,' said Ellie. 'But I bet I can figure it out eventually.'

'And if you don't,' said Cass, 'it won't be the end of the world. I mean, it's not like you need to draw hands to be a fashion designer. Unless you're designing gloves, of course,' she added.

'Hmm, I suppose I don't really care about designing gloves,' said Ellie. She was wearing a pair of tweed shorts she made herself. They are really cool, actually, though sometimes when she stood a certain way they looked a bit like a woollen nappy. But not much. I wonder if I could pay her to make a pair for me?

'When I started doing comics I just used to draw people with their hands behind their backs,' said Sam, running a hand through his hair. He'd had his hair cut but it was messy already. It's always a bit messy. His hands were all stained with charcoal. He always seems to be covered with some variety of art material. 'But I'm a bit better at drawing hands now. Well, I hope I am.'

We all instinctively looked at his picture, which was on the drawing table next to him.

'They look pretty hand-like to me,' said Cass.

'Thanks, Cass,' said Sam. He looked at his watch. 'Ah,

afraid I'd better go. I'm meeting Daire and some of the other lads from school in a few minutes.'

Most of the others had things to do too, so we all gathered up our stuff and strolled out. Everyone seemed to be going somewhere apart from me and Lucy, so we ended up walking towards the bus stop together.

'Do you know Sam's friends from school well?' I asked. She and Sam have been good friends since they were little, but they go to different schools now – he goes to St Anthony's with Richard (and John) and she goes to St Mary's.

'Oh yeah, his good friends,' she said. 'Daire's pretty cool. He's my friend too, I suppose. The three of us went to the Gaeltacht last summer, though this year Daire went back by himself 'cause we were at the camp.'

And I don't know why, but, without thinking, I found myself saying, 'Does Gemma get on with them? Sam's friends?'

Lucy looked very confused.

'Gemma?' said Lucy. 'Um, she's never met them, as far as I know. Why do you ask?'

'Oh, I just thought what with her and Sam being …' I said. 'You know.'

'Sam and Gemma?' said Lucy. Then realisation seemed to dawn on her. 'Oh, you thought they were … but there's nothing going on there!'

Now it was my turn to be surprised.

'But I thought ...' I said. 'After the camp party ... and I met you together in town a few weeks ago. I assumed they were together.'

'Oh no, nothing really happened,' said Lucy. 'I mean, they were with each other once at the end of the camp, but that was basically it. Sam thinks she's cool but he doesn't really fancy her. To be honest, I think he was a bit surprised when she kissed him.'

And that was it: the moment I realised I liked Sam. Because when she said that Sam didn't really fancy Gemma I felt a huge wave of relief wash over me and I couldn't really ignore it anymore.

'Really?' I said, trying to make my voice sound as normal as possible. I think I succeeded because Lucy didn't seem to notice anything strange.

'Oh yeah,' she said. 'In fairness to Sam, he doesn't usually mess girls around. If he'd known at the time that she really liked him, he wouldn't have kept kissing her back. I think he thought it was just, you know, the party mood – they were all just having fun.' As soon as she said this, Lucy looked horrified. 'Oh God, I shouldn't have told you she liked him.

It's not fair to her. Pretend I didn't say anything.'

'I actually did know already,' I admitted. 'Someone else told me.'

'Oh, okay.' Lucy looked relieved. 'So yeah. Basically, she told him that she really liked him and he says he turned her down gently, so I hope he did. He felt really bad, I do know that.'

'Really?' I said.

'Yeah,' said Lucy. 'He got worried he'd given her the impression he was into her earlier in the camp. She'd asked him whether something was going on between him and me, and of course he said there wasn't and there never had been. So then, when she declared her love, he got all worried that he'd somehow given her the wrong impression when he told her he was single. I'm pretty sure he didn't, though. I mean, I doubt he said, "Me and Lucy are just friends, but I'm actually looking for a girl who looks just like you", or something like that.'

I don't blame Gemma for thinking there might be something between Sam and Lucy. During the camp I actually wondered myself whether Lucy and Sam were really just good friends, and she had told me that people always thought this and that it was always very annoying when either of them ever liked somebody else.

'So how did you end up in town together, that time I met you?' I said. 'You and Sam and Gemma, I mean.'

'Oh, we just bumped into her when we were coming out of a bookshop,' said Lucy. 'It was a bit weird at first because Sam hadn't seen her since that night, but she seemed genuinely cool about everything and we ended up going for a coffee together. I don't think she's, like, pining away for him or anything.'

'Oh right,' I said. And then I didn't want to say anything else in case Lucy could tell what I was thinking about Sam. I didn't want to go on about him and his love life too much. Also, you know when you like someone and you feel really self-conscious mentioning their name? I was starting to feel like that – I was worried that I'd sound a bit funny when I said it and then Lucy would guess that I liked him. Because I definitely don't want her to know. In fact, I don't think I want anyone to know. So I asked some stupid random question about Maria Hanff and luckily by then we'd reached my bus stop, so we said goodbye.

But anyway. There it is. I like Sam. I really like him. And I'm not sure what I can do about it because I have no idea whether he likes me. I mean, I'm pretty sure he likes me as a friend because we get on well together and he lends me books and things. But that doesn't mean anything special, because he is someone who is used to being friends with girls as well as boys. For all I know he doesn't even fancy girls at all. Which I suppose would be better than him fancying another girl but not me. But still, I'd rather he liked girls. And by girls I just mean me.

Oh why is everything so complicated? Why did I have to start fancying Sam instead of just being friends with him? It would have been much easier. It's not like I was even looking for someone to fancy. But I can't help it. He's so nice and funny and he's very good at art. And he's cute. The more I see him, the cuter he looks. And he wears cool t-shirts. And I like the battered old boots he wears (even though they're a bit like John Kowalski's, but, in fairness, I liked John's boots too). And his new haircut is pretty cool. Oh I just like him. I really, really like him. And I'm so, so glad there's nothing going on between him and Gemma.

Though maybe I'm better off not even thinking about boys. If Rachel is anything to go by at the moment, no romance is worth it in the end. She is still feeling rotten. Jenny has just gone home after spending the entire day (as far as I can tell – she came over just when I was leaving the house to go to my practice) listening to Rachel being miserable. I need to think of something new to cheer her up tomorrow. I've been neglecting my plan to help her get over Tom. And, on a selfish note, it might stop me thinking about Sam.

SUNDAY ☼

I keep thinking about all the conversations I've had with Sam. He's always been really friendly and nice, but, as far as I can tell, he's always been friendly and nice to everyone he knows, male and female. He is the sort of person who just gets on with people. The only time I've ever seen him be a bit off was when he thought he was going to have to play Mr Banks in our production of *Mary Poppins*, and that's only because he gets a bit nervous on stage.

In fact, he was only expecting to be in the chorus when he joined up for the musical, but there were so few boys they had to give him the part of Uncle Albert. That made him nervous enough, which is why he was quite quiet during the rehearsals, but once he was actually performing he was pretty good. We only talked properly for the first time after the first triumphant night of the musical, when he was a lot more relaxed, and that was when I realised how nice he was. Though I didn't fancy him. And now I do. How did that happen?

Anyway, I haven't just been thinking about myself and my romantic problems (if you can count fancying someone you're friends with and who may not fancy you at all as an actual romantic problem). I've been thinking about Rachel too. I have been looking up ways to help someone get over a break-up online, but unfortunately it hasn't been very useful so far. One website suggested that I get Rachel to join me on a 5K run. I suppose running might do her some good, but I'm not willing to run 5K myself. I mean, it's not that I don't want to put myself out for Rachel, but I don't think it's actually possible for me to run five whole kilometres. I'm not even very good at just running around all the bases when we play rounders in PE.

The same website also suggested I get Rachel to help 'remodel my sitting room' which I presume means redecorate it. Actually, I wouldn't mind redecorating our sitting room – I keep telling Mum we should get rid of the boring cream paint on the walls and paint them a nice bright turquoise or something. And I wish we had a new couch. Ours is about a million years old and one of the arms has never been the same since me and Rachel played gymnastics on it too enthusiastically when I was nine. But sadly Mum and Dad refuse to listen to me, so I don't think they'd let me do up the room, even if it was in the good cause of helping Rachel.

The last tip suggested that we go on a 'girlfriends road trip', which isn't much use to me. I am fairly sure a walk around the teacher-training college doesn't count as a road trip, but in fairness I'm not sure what else I can do, given that we are both in school and can't drive. At least I managed to get her out of the house for an hour.

Anyway, all these tips seem to be designed for a sporty grown-up with lots of money and her own house and a car. In other words, the opposite of me. But surely there must be more useful tips out there. I will keep looking for inspiration.

LATER

I had no intention of persuading Rachel to join me on a run, but just out of interest while I was helping Mum empty the dishwasher this evening I asked her about doing 5K. She goes for runs sometimes, but it's mostly when I'm at school, so I sort of forget that she ever does them.

'I'd never be able to do that, would I?' I said. 'I mean, that's for serious runners.'

'I can run 5K!' said Mum. 'That's what I do pretty much

every time I go for a run!'

'What?' I said in astonishment. I'd sort of assumed she just went for a short trot around the block, not miles and miles and miles.

'Yes!' she said. 'It's only about half an hour!'

That puts a different light on things. If my ancient mother can run that far, surely I could do it too? Well, Rachel could anyway. I'm not sure I actually want to try. Besides, I don't have any proper running runners. I just have three different pairs of Converse and, even though I'm not a running expert, I know they are a lot less sturdy than the ones my Mum wears.

LATER

Spot is still glowing, by the way. When will my face go back to normal? When?

MONDAY ☀

I haven't told either Cass or Alice about how I feel about Sam.

I'm not sure why. When I liked Paperboy, I certainly went on about it enough. And Cass kept telling me she knew I fancied John Kowalski long before I actually did fancy him (though, in that case, it took me a while to accept I liked him because I was still pining for Paperboy). Now I come to think about it, Sam is the second boy whose charms just kind of grew on me. Maybe I am just not very good at figuring out exactly what, or indeed who, I want?

Anyway, I don't want to say anything about it right now. I really have no idea whether he fancies me back or not, and there is a good chance he doesn't. But if my friends know I fancy him, I'll feel like there is more pressure – well, not quite pressure, but they'll want to know what's happening and the answer will probably be 'nothing at all' and then I'll feel a bit stupid, even though they would never want me to feel like that.

But I think the main reason I don't really want to tell anyone is that then, if nothing ever happens or, which would be much worse, if he actually just tells me he doesn't fancy me, no one will feel sorry for me. Which I would hate. If no one knows and nothing ever happens then I will still be sad, but I wouldn't be embarrassed. And I know I shouldn't be embarrassed about this, and I know my friends really wouldn't think differently about me if they knew I liked someone who didn't like me, but I think I would still feel crap. So I will keep it to myself for now.

Of course, a part of me is dying to tell them. Mostly because I keep wanting to talk about him, and I don't really have a good excuse at the moment. We were sitting out on the playing fields during lunch today, partly because the weather was surprisingly warm and sunny and partly because we were avoiding Vanessa and Karen. Karen and Bernard's drama group actually does sometimes provide actors for films and plays and, yes, ads, so Karen seems to think she will be the next Kookie. What a terrible thought. Though to be honest, and I can't believe I'm saying this, I'd rather she became famous than Vanessa. I mean, Karen has shown she actually has a soul and some humanity buried deep down inside her. Vanessa hasn't. And Bernard the Fairytale Prince is quite decent really.

Anyway, when Karen first mentioned her intention to look for auditions the other week, I thought Vanessa would be more bothered by her and Bernard's dreams of fame, but now she clearly thinks that she is already so successful and famous that there's no chance of Karen stealing her thunder, so when Karen told us all about how she and Bernard had asked their drama teacher Sarah about auditions, Vanessa started patronising her instead.

'I'll be happy to give you and Bernard some tips on the craft,' she said today. 'Consider me your mentor.'

'You're an inspiration, Vanessa!' said Karen.

Sometimes, I don't know which of them's worse, I really don't. Oh, okay, I do. It's Vanessa.

Anyway, after a few minutes of listening to this, Cass, Alice, Ellie, Emma and I couldn't bear it anymore, so we escaped from the classroom and went out to lie on the grass with our sandwiches.

Ellie started talking about the art studio and how she loves having all that space to draw.

'The only downside,' she said, 'is that it makes the crappy little desk in my bedroom seem even smaller.'

'Can't you use that big table in your kitchen?' said Alice. Ellie's house is an average-sized, three-bedroom redbrick on Home Farm Road, but it has a great kitchen extension and in it there is a lovely big old table that looks like something from a country farm house.

Ellie sighed.

'My mum's always using it for her own projects,' she said. 'And besides, I can't leave stuff on it because we still have to use it as, like, an eating table. So it's just easier to draw in my room and not have to think about tidying away my stuff every two minutes because dinner's ready or Mum wants to make another goddess head-dress.'

And even though there was no need to mention him, I found myself saying, 'Sam said it made him want his own studio too.'

As soon as I said his name, I could feel my face getting a bit hot and I was sure I must have been bright red, but no one seemed to notice anything. And, believe me, if there was anything to notice, one of them would have said something. I haven't forgotten the way Cass carried on when she was sure I fancied John Kowalski (and, in fairness to her, she was right about that). But, in this case, I must have just sounded and looked totally normal, because Ellie just said, 'Yeah, we were talking about it on Saturday. He said he was working at the kitchen table last week and his sister plonked down a big glass of orange juice and nearly wrecked the comic he was working on. This is why we need proper studio space!'

'I love our practice space,' said Alice. 'And it's good to have an excuse to go into town.'

'I like not having to go all the way from the garage to your house in the rain whenever I need to go to the loo,' said Cass. 'Not that I'm ungrateful, Alice. Hey Dollface would not exist without your garage.'

'True,' said Alice. 'But I do prefer the Knitting Factory. And we'll get to see Kitty there on Saturday!'

'She'll be able to tell us the best way to end "Pistachio",' I said. 'Which is, of course, my and Alice's way.'

I really am excited about working with Kitty again. I can't wait until Saturday, and not just because I'll see Sam again. Now I come to think of it, I've started taking it for granted I'll see him there. Maybe he won't come every week. I mightn't see him for ages. I know I went for weeks on end without seeing him after the summer camp, but it's so weird, everything feels different now.

LATER

I suppose I could tell Rachel about the Sam stuff. She is surprisingly good at listening to my woes and giving advice in these situations – in fact, when John and I first kissed I told her about it before I told either Cass or Alice. But maybe she won't want to talk about love and romance now that her heart has been broken by evil Tom? It might be a bit insensitive. I don't remember any of the 'cheer up someone who's been dumped' articles telling me to go on about my own love problems.

EVEN LATER

I just did go to Rachel for advice, but it has nothing to do with my romance problems (unless it makes me so hideous no one can bear to look at me). My stupid spot is showing no signs of disappearing. It's still lurking under my skin, but it seems to be getting bigger and my chin actually feels sore. I stared at it for so long in the mirror, I started to worry it was actually swelling up before my very eyes, so I went in to Rachel to see what she thought.

'Is this spot getting bigger before your very eyes?' I asked.

Rachel stared at my chin for a minute.

'No,' she said. 'It's just a lurker. Everyone gets them. Just be glad it's not on your nose.'

Some comfort she is. I did weirdly feel a bit better though.

'So it's normal?' I said.

'As normal as anything about you could be,' she said. 'Yes, it's normal. It'll go eventually. Here, use this on it.'

And she took out her little tube of expensive spot gel and handed it to me.

'This should calm it down a bit,' she said. She is not too bad, really. Maybe I will tell her about the Sam stuff soon.

TUESDAY ☾

I feel ashamed of myself. Clearly I have no principles. Today at lunchtime Vanessa produced a big bag full of boxes of Blue-bird Bakery Yummy Scrummy Cookies.

'Share these among yourselves,' she commanded, handing around packets emblazoned with the Bluebird Bakery logo. Her loyal chums joined in.

'They're really good!' said Caroline, handing me an open packet of cookies.

'Oh, thanks,' I said, and took it. It felt rude not to accept. But once I had the packet, it felt hypocritical to eat the cook-ies after all the time I've spent giving out about Vanessa and the ad. My friends felt the same way.

'It just doesn't feel right,' said Alice quietly. 'I mean, we hate the ad ...'

'And we don't like Vanessa much either,' said Emma.

On the other side of the room, Vanessa was saying some-thing about being a 'Bluebird Brand Ambassador'.

'They do look like nice cookies, though,' said Ellie. We looked into the box. They did look nice, all big and fresh and crunchy. 'Aw, I don't care, I'm going to try one.' She got out a cookie and took a big bite.

'Well?' said Cass.

'Whoah,' said Ellie. 'That is one delicious cookie. Seriously, it's really good. I'm going to have another one. Sorry.'

Cass sighed.

'Oh go on then, pass one over,' she said.

A few moments later, we were all eating them. And Ellie was right, they were totally delicious. Much nicer than any of the chocolate chip cookies my parents usually buy. Not that our house is ever full of biscuits. My parents are very stingy when it comes to buying delicious treats. No wonder I have to make my own fudge.

Of course, Vanessa soon marched over to see what we thought.

'Well, aren't they the best cookies you've ever tasted?' she said.

And much as it pained me to agree with her, I had to say, 'Yeah, they're really good.'

'They're gorgeous,' said Alice. Everyone agreed.

Vanessa, unsurprisingly, looked very smug.

'I knew you'd all like them,' she said. 'I'm going to be handing them out at special public appearances soon – in character as Kookie, of course. She's really taking off. People are even dressing up as her now.'

We all stared at her. Had she finally gone mad? Surely no one loved the ads so much they were actually trying to be Kookie? But I'm afraid it's true. I have now seen it with my own eyes. It turns out that the Bluebird Bakery asked people to send in videos and pictures of themselves being 'a little bit kooky' and lots of people have obeyed this irritating request.

There is now a whole page full of videos and photos of people prancing around with small dogs and musical instruments, wearing frilly frocks and drinking tea out of old-fashioned cups. One girl sent a photo of herself knitting some rainbow-striped socks next to a Yorkshire Terrier which was wearing a little bonnet. This looks like animal cruelty to me (the bonnet part, not the knitting socks part). At least Handsome Dan performed naked, as nature intended him to be.

Of course, there is nothing wrong with all the activities in these photos and videos, apart from dressing up animals in outfits (and, in fairness, the Yorkshire Terrier didn't seem to mind much – it wasn't as if the bonnet was hurting him). As I said, I like most of these things. In fact, now I really wish I could knit my own socks because it not only looks fun – you knit the sock as a sort of tube with five pointy needles – but you get a nice cosy pair of socks at the end of it. But when you make a big deal of how kooky these activities (and dogs) supposedly are, then they become extremely annoying. I am not sure why this is. It is quite mysterious.

Anyway, Vanessa thinks the photos and videos are all a tribute to her own brilliance, and I suppose they are, depressingly enough. I mean, people do seem to love that ad. But that doesn't mean I've got to encourage her egomania by eating her hand-outs. If she brings in more biscuits, I must stay strong and tell her I'm not hungry. Maybe I could write some song lyrics about the importance of staying true to your beliefs, no matter how difficult it is? It would encourage not just myself but other people too. We were messing around with a possible new song on Saturday – it sort of has a tune, so I could try and work out some lyrics to fit it.

LATER

I have written some lyrics. Every time I'm tempted to be a huge hypocrite and take Vanessa's cookies, I will sing it (just in my head, obviously – I'm not going to start suddenly singing in public).

You know the right thing to do

You know what you stand for
But then something is offered to you
And it's too good to ignore.
CHORUS
It doesn't matter
How tasty it will be
Because what tastes better
Is honesty.

I think it has potential. I'd like to incorporate a great word I found in my rhyming dictionary to rhyme with 'do' – it is 'smew' and it is a sort of diving duck. I've got some good bird and animal lyrics from the dictionary before, like when I compared John Kowalski to a 'tercel', which is a sort of hawk. Though he does have a bird of prey air about him, and I'm not quite sure how I could fit diving ducks into this song. 'You're avoiding problems like a smew'? I will think about it some more.

WEDNESDAY ✿

Just three more days until I see Sam again. It's a bit sad to be thinking about it, but I can't help it. I hope I don't act all weird. Or that he doesn't march in talking about how he's just met the love of his life or something. Maybe he'll suddenly fall for Ellie. Or Cass. Or Alice. Not that he'd have much luck with any of them.

School wasn't too bad today. Vanessa was no more annoying than usual (which obviously still means she was quite annoying, but we're used to that), and Miss Kelly was in a surprisingly jovial mood, even though she spent a lot of the class talking about the environmental consequences of urban expansion. And Mrs Harrington was even more cheerful – when we were leaving our English class for lunch, she told me she's sent her book off to a literary agent. Or at least the first few chapters of it.

'It's called *The Road Through the Bluebells*,' she said proudly. 'And it's about a woman in a small Irish town who decides she wants to be a gardener.'

It doesn't sound very exciting to me, but then neither do my mum's books and loads of people love them. So maybe Mrs Harrington will actually be a big success. I don't think it's very likely, I'm afraid. Though if this does happen, we might get a new English teacher who isn't obsessed with my mother, which would be a very good thing. Still, even Mrs Harrington doesn't annoy me as much as she did a year ago. Maybe I have become a more patient and noble person?

In other news, the lurker has finally burst forth. It looks hideous but is strangely less sore. Now I must just let it take its course (hopefully aided by that posh spot stuff) and make sure I don't touch it. And I must resist the temptation to squeeze it, because I don't want to be scarred for life. I'm just hoping it will have passed its peak and started to fade away by Saturday. I don't want Sam to think I'm covered in boils too.

THURSDAY ◎

Oh dear. I was right again. And I sort of wish I wasn't.

I mean that I was right when I told Rachel I thought Dad was going too far in his attempts to jazz up Henry Higgins. Obviously I am often right about other things too. I'm right about where to end 'Pistachio' (sorry, Cass), I was right about Vanessa getting the ad, and then I was right about the ad being the worst thing that has ever been shown on television, and I was right when I dumped John Kowalski. But in all those cases I was glad that I was right. And I am not glad about Dad turning into a sort of deranged show off. It's one thing seeing him dance around when it's part of the actual show. It's quite another watching him add his own bits.

This is how I found out. The hall hasn't found a new class to fill that spare slot, so the musical society are still having two rehearsals a week. As usual on *My Fair Lady* nights, I had got my homework done nice and early so I could enjoy the luxury of lying on the couch and watching telly without my parents coming in and insisting on turning over to something boring like the news, or making stupid and unfunny comments about whatever programme I'm trying to enjoy. I had just turned on the TV when my mum rang the landline. Rachel was upstairs on the phone to Jenny (again) so I answered it.

'Oh Bex, it's you,' she said. 'I'm afraid I need you to do something for me.'

'What is it?' I said, suspiciously.

'I left my dance shoes at home and we're blocking a scene at the moment so your dad and I really can't go home and get them. Could you pop down here with them?'

'Mum!' I said. 'It's miles away!' Which is only a tiny little bit of an exaggeration.

'Don't be ridiculous, Rebecca,' said Mum. 'It's a ten-minute walk. Fifteen at the very most. Please!'

'Why can't Rachel do it?' I said.

'Because she's had a very hard time recently,' said Mum.

157

'And by the time I persuade her to do it the rehearsal will be over. Come on, Rebecca!'

'Will you give me money so I can get a nice sandwich after band practice on Saturday?' I said, cunningly exploiting this rare moment of weakness.

'Oh, you've resorted to demanding bribes, have you?' said Mum. 'Alright, you win. I will give you sandwich money. Now, get down here with those shoes! They're in a bag in the hall.'

'Okay,' I said. 'I'll see you down there.'

I yelled up the stairs to tell Rachel I was leaving, grabbed the shoes and headed down to the hall where the musical society practise. It actually is just about a kilometre away, but it feels longer when you were planning to spend the evening sitting on a sofa watching telly instead of walking along Gracepark Road.

When I arrived at the hall, the cast were in the middle of a scene so I didn't want to interrupt. I just slipped in and took a seat at the back of the room. The cast were just starting the scene in which Alfred Dolittle, the dustman and father of the heroine, Eliza, is singing down the pub with all his dustman pals about getting married in the morning. Of course, Henry Higgins is not meant to be in this scene because he is a posh person who is trying to turn Eliza into a fancy lady and he doesn't hang around in pubs with Edwardian bin men. But as the actor playing Alfred strutted about the stage with his pub pals (including my mother, who was waving around a bunch of paper flowers in a very suggestive manner), suddenly Dad appeared at the side of the stage.

He strolled on casually, holding a notebook, looking intrigued by the dancing Cockneys before him. At first, he just stood there and pretended to take some notes in his notebook. And then slowly he began to sort of dance around in the background. When the main performers in the scene sang a particularly cheerful or funny line, he pretended to laugh. When all the people in the pub were dancing around arm in arm, he gave a few twirls on his own. Every so often, he'd incorporate the note-taking into his moves – he'd sort of wave around his pen in time to the music and then pretend to write in the book.

At one stage, he jumped up on a chair in order to observe the main performers more closely and did a little dance on it. His dancing was pretty skillful and he moved in perfect time to the music, but it was all a bit, well, weird. Very weird. The longer it went on, the more insane it looked. And yet I couldn't look away.

When Alfred Dolittle had sung his final line and the scene

was over at last, a small woman with red hair who was clearly Laura, the director, said, 'Very good, everyone, especially for a first run-through of a scene! Joe, you really captured Alfred's cheekiness, but maybe we could have some more energy in the dancing?'

Joe, who looked quite breathless after all his leaping around, nodded and said, 'Okay, Laura.'

'Now, chorus,' said Laura. 'I think we need to be a bit more expressive. Do you know what I mean?'

I certainly did. I don't want to boast, but even the director of *Mary Poppins* acknowledged that I was very good at acting-while-singing when I was a member of the chorus. But some of these chorus members were barely sing-acting at all. They might as well just have been in a choir. Not my mother, I might add. She's pretty good. In fact, I think she should have got a better part in the show. Maybe the woman playing Henry Higgins's housekeeper will have a heart attack like the man who was playing the Beadle in the last show and Mum will have to step in and take over her part? Not that I actually want the poor woman to have a heart attack, of course. But if she's ever going to have one, she might as well have it now.

Anyway, after Laura had given a few more notes to the cast she turned to Dad and I found myself feeling very nervous. It was one thing me thinking he'd gone too far with his dancing, but it was another to hear the director giving out to him. But that didn't happen.

'Now, Ed,' she said. 'That was ... very original. Can you tell me a bit more about your, um, motivation?'

'Well,' said Dad. 'Henry is an observer of society. He's always on the outside, looking in. And by having him enter this scene we show how he can observe the world that Eliza comes from, but never really join it.'

He looked very pleased. The rest of the cast looked a little less pleased.

'Oh, okay,' said Laura. She looked a bit unsure of herself. 'Well, your dancing was very good.'

And that was it! I remembered what Mum had said about the old director, Dearbhla, being a lot more tough. I bet she'd have told him to calm down. But it looks like Laura is too scared to stand up to him!

'Right, we'll take a few minutes' break,' said Laura. 'Then let's have a run-through of Eliza's first song, okay?'

Dad immediately went off to what looked like the loo at the far end of the hall before I had a chance to get his attention, but Mum had noticed and waved at me, while Laura was giving her notes, and came straight over to me.

'Here are your shoes,' I said, handing over the bag.

'Thanks, love,' said Mum. 'Did you see much of the scene?'

'Pretty much all of it,' I said. 'Um, it was very good.'

There was a pause. I knew we were both thinking of Dad, but neither of us quite knew what to say about him.

Finally, Mum said, 'Your dad's really working hard on Henry Higgins, isn't he?'

'Um, yes,' I said. 'But it's a bit … well, it's a bit … isn't it? I mean, don't the other actors mind him jumping in? He's not even meant to be in that scene, at least not in the film.'

'Well, they're just workshopping things at the moment,' said Mum diplomatically. 'That was the first run-through of the scene. I'm sure there'll be a few changes before the actual performances.'

Then Laura called, 'Right, everyone, can I have Eliza and the chorus on stage, please?' and Mum said, 'I'd better go! Thanks for the shoes, love. I'll see you at home.'

I was almost tempted to stay for a while to find out whether Dad had managed to shove himself into this scene too, but I know visitors aren't meant to sit in on rehearsals (no one was really allowed into the hall when we were rehearsing *Mary Poppins*), so I slipped out again. But as I walked home, I couldn't help thinking about what I'd just witnessed. I think

Laura needs to stand up to Dad more. Otherwise, she has created a monster. Now Dad has basically been handed official permission to give Henry Higgins a bit more oomph, there will be no stopping him. I saw the gleam in his eye when he leapt up on that chair. He'll take over the entire show unless she does something!

And if he does, I can't imagine the rest of the cast will be too pleased. But I'm afraid there's nothing I can do about it. I'll just hope someone, preferably Dad, sees sense. Though I am not optimistic. There's no way he's going to be satisfied playing Henry Higgins in the traditional way. When I got home, I told Rachel what I'd witnessed. As I'd hoped, it distracted her from her moping – I mean, misery.

'But what was everyone else doing while he was prancing about the place?' she asked.

'Just getting on with the song,' I said. 'I think they were trying to ignore him.'

'That's pretty professional of them,' said Rachel. 'For an amateur musical society. I mean, I don't think I could concentrate on doing a song if Dad was jumping around on chairs in the background.'

'Well, I don't think they'll put up with it forever,' I said. 'I don't think I would. It'll drive them mad.'

Oh, I wish Dad could be content just playing Henry Higgins normally. This will all end in tears. He's like Icarus! He's going to fly too close to the sun and then fall down to earth. Or at least get booted out of his role as Henry Higgins.

The only good thing is that, even though we were both a bit worried about Dad's transformation into deranged diva (or whatever the male equivalent of a diva is. Maybe there isn't one? That's a bit sexist), it definitely took Rachel's mind off her problems. In fact, she seemed quite like her old self. Which is a good thing.

FRIDAY ☺

I knew I shouldn't have taken Vanessa's cookies. It definitely encouraged her. Today she turned up with a bag full of Kookie badges. There is a sort of cartoon drawing of her face and the words 'Have Yourself a Kooky Little Day' on them. Unsurprisingly, no one in my class, apart from Karen and Caroline, was eager to go around sporting a badge with Vanessa on it, but she was handing them out all over school, and by the time we left at half three I saw loads of girls wearing them. It was as though Vanessa had become the leader of a terrible cult. God knows what she'll do next. Hand out t-shirts? Force everyone to sing her song? I think I heard her say something at lunch about being on the radio next week, but I'm hoping I imagined it.

And all the teachers were being annoying too. They keep going on about 'knuckling down' and studying hard. Even Mrs Harrington got all fired up about it. And Frau O'Hara kept telling us how important it was to have a good German vocabulary 'because it's no use knowing the grammar if you don't know any words'. I am not sure if I know enough grammar OR words. In fact, now I'm starting to feel panicky about the exams already and they're not for months and months.

But just the thought of studying all the time makes me feel tired. I need to find fun ways to motivate myself. Maybe I will ask Alice to let me practise my German on her. We could always try doing an entire band practice in German! Though as I don't even know the German for drums, I am not sure it would work very well.

On a more positive note, last night I found another list of things to do for a friend (or sister) who has been dumped, and as they don't all involve cars or sportiness or vast amounts of money I can actually do some of them. One of the suggested cheering methods was 'make her something tasty' and while I am not exactly a master chef, I have definitely mastered the art of making delicious fudge. So after school today, Cass came over and helped me make a batch of the white chocolate variety just for Rachel. I even bought posh white chocolate, which cost all that I had left of my pocket money – that is the sort of sacrifice I am willing to make for my sister's happiness.

I said this to Cass and she said, 'Calm down, Bex. It was only €1.50. You're not donating a kidney.'

No one appreciates my kindness, not even my supposed best friends.

'Well, it's €1.50 I could have spent on myself!' I said. 'AND I'm making her some special white chocolate fudge!'

'So am I,' said Cass, waving the wooden spoon. 'Can I at least have a few pieces myself?'

'We both can,' I said. 'I mean, there's only so much fudge Rachel can eat herself.'

'Where is she, anyway?' asked Cass, as we started measuring out the ingredients. We are so experienced at this stage we can almost do it without checking the exact amounts in the cookery book (but we do always check, just to be on the safe side).

'She went to Jenny's after school,' I said, getting out the condensed milk. I wonder if condensed milk is used for anything besides making fudge. And how do you condense milk anyway? 'But she's not staying late because Jenny's going to the theatre with her parents tonight. So she'll be back to eat her fudge while it's fresh.'

While the fudge was cooling, we went up to my room. I put on some music fairly loud so nobody could hear what we were talking about. I know my mother claims she isn't spying on us, looking for inspiration for her teen fiction, but it's better to be safe than sorry. We lolled on my bed and had a good conversation about how much we were looking forward to our workshop with Kitty, and about the future of the band.

'I know I am biased,' said Cass. 'And obviously I wouldn't say this to anyone but you or Alice because it would just look like mad boasting, but I genuinely think I'd like Hey Dollface if I wasn't, like, in it. I mean, we've got a lot better over the last year.'

She's right. I, too, would actually like to listen to our songs even if I hadn't co-written them. I never thought we'd turn out to be good at writing tunes and riffs and lyrics and stuff, but I really think we have, and the summer camp helped a lot.

'Just think,' I said, 'a year ago I could barely play my drums.'

'Sadly some things haven't changed,' said Cass. 'I'm joking! I'm joking!'

But I threw a pillow at her anyway.

167

I almost told her about liking Sam, but then I thought it might make me even more self-conscious tomorrow so I didn't. It was fun just sitting around talking rubbish, though. Sometimes it is nice to be reminded that, even though she and Alice are going out with people now, our friendship hasn't changed. I know I haven't told them about Sam yet, but I know that if I really needed to talk to them I always could, because we are always there for each other. Not that I would ever say something so cheesy to either of them, of course.

After a while, my mum stuck her head in the door to say she was going into town to give Dad a lift home because someone had blocked his car in the college car park and he couldn't get it out.

'Why can't he get the bus?' I said.

'Because he's got a huge pile of essays to read through this weekend,' said Mum, 'and he can't carry them on the bus.'

I don't see why not. They can't be that heavy. I have to lug a giant school bag full of books around every day AND I walk to school so I don't even get to sit down on a bus for some of my journey. But if it got Mum out of the house for a while I wasn't going to complain.

After she left, we went down to check on the fudge and if I say so myself, it was our finest yet. The white chocolate is definitely a winner. We put some in a container for Cass to take home and put most of the squares on a big plate to wait for Rachel's return. Though of course we kept aside a few squares to eat now.

'I'm not joking,' said Cass, in between chews. 'I really think we could sell this. If we had, like, all the legal food-making-and-selling stuff sorted out.'

'That might take a while,' I said. 'I can't imagine we'll ever get any of our kitchens up to professional standards.'

'Well, don't rule it out,' said Cass. 'Ooh, is that the door?'

It was, and a moment later Rachel came into the kitchen. She looked a bit tired.

'Oh, hi,' she said. 'What have you been doing?'

'Making fudge,' I said. 'For you!'

Rachel stared at me.

'Seriously?' she said.

'Yes!' I said. 'It's all for you!' I pointed to the plate of fudge squares. Luckily, it wasn't obvious that we had eaten quite a lot of fudge already.

'Wow,' said Rachel. She looked genuinely quite amazed. 'Um, thanks Bex. And Cass.' I don't know why she seemed surprised by my great kindness and generosity. It's not like I'm normally a total monster (am I?). Anyway, she looked very pleased, as well as surprised, so my mission to cheer her up actually worked. And she looked even more pleased when she tasted her special treat.

'This is really good!' she said.

I suppose I should have been modest, but I just said, 'I know.' Which was horribly smug of me, as Rachel pointed out. Still, she didn't seem to mind too much. The three of us ended up sitting around the table talking for a while. Rachel said Mum had shown her the cover of the new Ruthie book this morning.

'You'd just left to go to school when the publishers sent it over,' she said.

'Is it as bad as the last one?' I said, thinking of the pouty girl on the first Ruthie cover.

'Hmm, about the same,' said Rachel. 'It's got a picture of Ruthie – at least I presume it's meant to be Ruthie – standing there with her arms folded and one eyebrow raised, looking all sassy. Like she's handing out her rules for life.'

'Oh dear,' I said miserably. I could imagine this only too well.

'I know,' said Rachel. 'I have to say, I think that ridiculous Vanessa girl in your class would be perfect for the part. If they ever do make it into a film or a TV show, which I hope they don't. It'd only encourage Mum to write more.'

'Though wouldn't it be worth it if it made her really rich?' said Cass.

Rachel and I thought about it. Would it be worth getting to go on a holiday that didn't involve sleeping in a tent in France if it meant more Ruthie AND possibly Vanessa becoming famous? We couldn't decide.

It was actually a pretty cool evening, and for once Rachel didn't act like we were babies, which is usually how she behaves when my friends are over. It was like we were the same age, sort of. Maybe the older you get, the less age gaps matter? I mean, I'm fifteen now, and Cass will be fifteen next week (which reminds me, I need to get her a present tomorrow). We are practically grown up already.

SATURDAY ☺

Oh, what a day. I am a bit confused but in a good way. A very good way. At least, I think it's good.

We had booked our practice for one o'clock, and to show my parents that the band isn't interfering with my schoolwork I actually did some homework before I left. I called my parents into my room so they could see that I was doing maths and not just lying on my bed listening to music and reading something for fun, which I must admit is what I'm normally doing on Saturday mornings.

'Well done,' said Mum, but she didn't seem particularly impressed. She seemed to think I should be doing this anyway and that it wasn't a big deal. Still, I'm glad I did it (and not just because I showed my parents that I can combine music and scholarly life, but because now I actually have most of my homework done and it's not hanging over me until Sunday evening like it usually is).

Anyway, Alice's mum was going to a friend's house in Drumcondra so she dropped Alice off at mine and we got the bus in together. I felt like we hadn't seen each other on our own for a while. Cass and I go to each other's houses more often in the evenings because she lives quite near me, but it's a much bigger deal for Alice to get anywhere, what with her living in the middle of nowhere. So it was kind of nice to just hang out with her for a while, even if we were just sitting on a 16 bus for most of it. I almost told Alice about Sam, but then I thought it would make me very self-conscious if we bumped into him as soon as we arrived at the Knitting Factory. So instead, we talked about school and telly and books we were reading and stuff. And then we got talking about her and Richard and how good it was to go out with someone who she could talk to properly about band stuff.

Then Alice said, 'Bex ... do you still think about Paperboy?'

And when she asked me, I realised that I don't. I mean, seriously, hardly ever. In fact, I don't think I've thought about him once all week, which might be a record.

'Not really,' I said. 'I suppose he comes into my head sometimes. But it's definitely not like it used to be.'

'It just shows you can get over everything,' said Alice, but she didn't say it in a 'I told you so' way. It was in a kind way, and it was a very cheering thought. If you'd told me back in January that I wouldn't be crying over Paperboy all the time, I simply wouldn't have believed you. I never thought I'd be totally happy again, or at least I never thought I'd stop thinking about Paperboy all the time. But there you go. I have actually moved on. I suppose you can get over pretty much anything.

I was still feeling pleased about this when we arrived at the Knitting Factory and found Cass and Liz talking to Tall Paula from Exquisite Corpse. It was great to see them all.

'I didn't realise you'd got a practice space here!' I said to Liz.

'Neither did I until this morning!' she said. 'We got a cancellation. We've been on the waiting list since it started, but all you summer-camp people had first dibs. Which is fair enough.'

'Hey, look who it is,' said Cass.

I turned and saw three boys around our age. They were all wearing impressively outlandish garments – one was wearing a fur coat, cycling shorts and a sort of floral bum bag. They looked vaguely familiar, but it took me a few moments to realise who they were. Then it hit me.

'It's Puce!' I said in surprise. The boys glanced over and waved, looking a bit shy. I definitely recognised them now. They had been on the summer camp, and when it started they were all wearing cardigans and played their instruments while staring shyly at their feet. But, by the end, thanks to some lessons in stagecraft from Shane Driscoll, the lead singer of The Invited, they were strutting around the stage in leather trousers and jumpsuits. It was quite a transformation. And it looks like they've kept up their commitment to eye-catching ensembles. They came over to say hello properly.

'We've got a workshop with Shane today,' said Niall, the lead singer. He was wearing a bomber jacket in a sort of Hawaiian pattern. It was very colourful.

'We've got one with Kitty,' said Alice. 'Oh look, there she is!'

It was so, so cool to see Kitty again. We hadn't seen her at all since the camp ended. Puce and Paula knew her from the camp, of course, because she'd taught all of them in the big workshops, but we introduced her to Liz and they all talked about guitar pedals for a minute until Kitty remembered she was meant to be mentoring us, so we told the others we'd see them later in the art space and we took her off to our practice room.

'This place is VERY cool, guys,' she said. 'Now show me what you've been doing here.'

We played a couple of our newish songs, including of course 'Pistachio'.

We finished that one by repeating the chorus a few times (which is, of course, Cass's favourite approach). Then Alice said, 'We've been having some trouble with the ending ...'

'Alice and I think it should end suddenly, straight after the last chorus,' I said.

'But I think we should repeat the chorus a few times,' said Cass. 'What do you think?'

'I can't tell you what to do with your songs, people!' laughed Kitty.

'We really do need outside input, though,' I said.

'Hmmm,' said Kitty. 'Okay. Well, I see what you're going for, Cass, but let me hear it the other way. Just run through the last chorus and end there.'

We did. Kitty looked thoughtful. 'I think that works better, to be honest. It's tighter. But it's still up to you.'

Alice and I looked at Cass, who rolled her eyes but conceded defeat in a good-natured fashion.

I knew I was right about that song! Though Kitty did say later that 'there's no right or wrong when it comes to music. It's all subjective. But it's about finding out what works best for you.'

Anyway, she stayed in the studio with us for a whole hour and it was really great. I'd almost forgotten how good she was at making us feel all enthusiastic and full of energy. And she showed Alice how to do a really cool thing with an effect pedal she'd never used before, which was awesome. But the coolest thing was that she told us she and the other mentors have been talking to Veronica and we can start doing afternoon gigs in the Knitting Factory in a couple of weeks! About three or four bands will be playing at each one, so we won't be doing really long sets, but it'll still be the first time we'll have played more than five songs in public. I can't wait.

After Kitty left, we had another hour of practice time left, so we tried out her suggestions and they all worked really well. Before we started playing 'Ever Saw in You' with added pedal effects, I remembered my great studying idea and suggested that we try talking in German for a bit, but Cass refused.

'You can't just spring the idea of talking in another language on me like that with no warning,' she said. 'I need to psychologically prepare myself.'

'Oh, alright,' I said. 'Maybe next week, then. What's the German for drum, anyway, Alice?'

'Um, Schlagzeug, I think,' said Alice.

Apparently Schlagzeug literally means 'hit-thing', as in a thing for hitting. Good grief. But what can you expect from a language where the word for glove is 'Handschuh', which just means 'hand shoe'? Anyway, eventually Cass reluctantly agreed to do some German speaking next Saturday after I pointed out how useful it would be to know how to talk about music 'auf Deutsch' if we ever went on tour in Germany.

'Or Austria,' said Alice helpfully. 'Or bits of Switzerland.'

When our time was up, we went back to the art space to meet the others. As soon as I saw Sam, I felt a strange fluttery butterfly feeling in my tummy. I was really glad he was there, but I also felt weirdly nervous. It felt like everything had changed since I saw him last week, like I wouldn't know how to talk to him normally now. Luckily, so many people were there – Senan, Liz and her bandmate Katie, Paula and her bandmate Sophie, Ellie and Lucy, the Puce boys – that I didn't have to say anything to him straight away besides 'Hi', which gave me time to collect myself.

In fact, after a while, I started to worry that I wouldn't get to talk to him at all today. Everyone was sitting around the art room chatting and drinking cans of fizzy drinks or cups of coffee and tea from the tiny studio kitchen. But I was on one side of the room with Cass and Liz, next to Katie and the Puce boys, who were talking very enthusiastically about bass amps. Sam was right on the other side of the room talking to Senan, Ellie and Paula, and I couldn't figure out a way of getting to talk to him, without it looking totally obvious. At one stage, he caught my eye and raised a hand in a 'hello!' sort of mini-wave, but that wasn't exactly an invitation to march across the room to join him.

So I kept talking to the others, even though I was hyper aware of Sam on the other side of the room with his messy hair and his scruffy old shirt and cords and boots and his nice hands (he has such interesting hands) all covered with ink and charcoal. I was trying so hard not to look at him, I was worried I was making myself even more obvious. And, as time went on and we both stayed on opposite sides of the room, I got more and more depressed. I mean, I'd prepared myself for the possibility that he wouldn't be there at all, but not for the possibility that we could both be in the same room and not actually talk to each other. Eventually, everyone was sitting around sort of talking together, but that meant I still didn't get to talk to Sam on his own. All the excitement I'd had that morning seemed to drain away as it got later and later and we still hadn't said more than a few casual words to each other.

Then everyone started getting ready to leave. Cass and Liz were going to Liz's house, so they set off with Katie to get the bus on Nassau Street. Alice was meeting Richard, who hadn't been practising today because the Wicked Ways guitarist has gastric flu and is too sick to play the guitar. And Lucy has been thinking of learning how to sew so she was going home with Ellie, who was going to show her how to use her sewing machine (well, technically it's her mum's sewing machine, but Ellie uses it more than her mum does these days).

So basically, when everyone was saying goodbye to each other outside the Knitting Factory, Sam and I ended up being the only ones who didn't have anything to do straight away. I felt very self-conscious and I thought I should just get away before I said something stupid so I said, 'Well, I suppose I should …'

And then Sam said, 'Are you in a hurry to get home?'

And I said, 'Um, not really.'

'Do you want to go and get a coffee?' said Sam. 'Or whatever hot drink you like? To be honest, I'm not in a huge hurry to get home myself. My parents are repainting the kitchen and they'll just make me sandpaper skirting boards. And, besides, I haven't talked to you all afternoon.'

I could feel my tummy fluttering again, only this time it was with excitement. But I tried to sound completely casual.

'Yeah, sure,' I said. 'Where will we go? What about the Pepperpot?'

So that's where we went. Thank heaven Mum had given me extra sandwich money for bringing those shoes down to the hall. Imagine if I'd had to say, 'Sorry, Sam, I can't go out for a drink because I only have thirty-five cents in the world, apart from the money in my savings account, which my parents won't let me take out because they think I'll "waste it", whatever that means.'

Anyway, when we were sitting down at our table by the railings, I suddenly felt a bit awkward because I realised it was the first time Sam and I have actually gone anywhere together. I mean, we've talked loads, but it's always been in corridors and at bus stops and while walking down the street or sitting around in arts spaces. It's just been casual. But this all felt rather formal. Until then, I'd never found it difficult to talk to

Sam, but now I couldn't think of anything to say.

'Sooo,' I said, and then wished I hadn't, because I worried I sounded like I was nervous. Which I was. But luckily Sam didn't seem to notice anything weird. He just looked at the wool shop next to the café and said, 'Wow, I didn't realise wool came in so many colours. That display looks really cool. Like an art installation or something.' And then the waitress arrived and took our orders – hot chocolate (as usual) for me and a coffee for him.

'I should probably be cutting down on coffee,' he said. 'I find myself drinking loads of it at night when I'm working on my comics and then I end up wide awake at four in the morning.'

'Well, one won't hurt,' I said. 'It's only four o'clock in the afternoon.'

'Yeah, you're probably right,' he said. 'And it's really good coffee. Right, this is my last one of the day.'

'Do you find you work better at night?' I said. 'I don't mean homework, I mean, like, art or writing stuff. I think I do. I mean, sometimes I'll start writing something quite late and it's like I get a second wind. I just want to keep going even though I was tired earlier.'

'Yeah, me too,' said Sam. He paused. 'Although I suppose

181

that could be the coffee.'

Our drinks arrived, and then we stayed there for ages talking about loads of things, about art and writing and books and our annoying families. He talked about how people still don't think comics can be really great art, no matter how beautiful or serious they are. He pulled out a graphic novel from his bag by a writer and artist called Jaime Hernandez. The pictures were really brilliant.

'Ooh, is there a band in it?' I said, when I opened a page and saw a really cool picture of a girl holding a bass.

'There is. The stories are amazing,' said Sam. 'But will we ever study something like this in school? No, because not enough people realise that comics are proper art!'

I told him that I wanted to write funny books and they weren't given enough credit either.

'Let's drink a toast,' said Sam. 'To books that don't get the credit they deserve.' He raised his coffee cup and clinked it off my mug of hot chocolate. 'Just think,' he said. 'In thirty years maybe you'll be a really famous writer and I'll be a famous artist ...'

'And writer,' I said. 'Of comics.'

'And writer of comics,' said Sam. 'And you'll have won, I dunno. The Nobel Prize or the Booker or something. And I'll have won whatever you get for doing great comics.'

'And we'll both be, like, in your face, everyone who sneers at funny books and comics!' I said happily. Then I thought of something. 'Of course, I might also be an international rock star too. With Hey Dollface.'

'Meh, you can do that as well as the writing,' said Sam with a shrug. 'You could write on the tour bus. Or the private jet.'

He is so easy to talk to, about big ideas and little silly stuff. I've never really talked like that with a boy before. With Paperboy I never really had a chance because we were still kind of getting to know each other when he went away, and with John I spent most of the time just listening to his own grand plans and theories about life. But when I talk to Sam, it's like we're both into what the other person is saying. He actually makes me feel like I could become a famous writer. Or rock star. Or both.

We talked a bit about our families too. I told him about Rachel being dumped and how I was trying to cheer her up, and he said when his sister found out her boyfriend had left her for someone else she threw black paint all over a painting she'd been doing of him.

'And then she left it on his doorstep and never talked to him again,' said Sam. 'It was a bit over the top, to be honest. She's mortified about it now.'

'Rachel hasn't done anything like that,' I said. 'At least, I don't think so. Did your sister get over it eventually, then?'

'I suppose so,' said Sam. 'I mean, she seems okay now. In her head-wrecking way.'

We ended up staying there talking for over an hour. I was scared to look at my phone to check the time, in case Sam realised how late it was and decided he had to escape, but he didn't seem to be in a hurry. Eventually, though, my phone rang, and, unsurprisingly, it was my mother wondering where I was. I should have just texted her earlier to say I was hanging around town for a while.

'If you're not going to be home for dinner, I need to know!' said Mum crossly. 'Now, get home as soon as you can. And it was your turn to help do some hoovering today, too.'

If I had been with Alice or Cass or Jane, or someone else I'd been friends with for ages, I would have just argued back to her, but I didn't want to do that the first time Sam and I went somewhere on our own together, so I just said, 'Okay, I'll be home soon.' I turned to Sam. 'Yikes. I'd better be off.'

'Me too, I suppose,' said Sam. 'I hope they've done most of the sandpapering.'

So we paid and strolled off to our bus stops. We reached mine first, and as soon as we got there a bus turned up so we just said bye quickly and I jumped on it. And that was that.

Of course, now I keep going back over the conversation and worrying if I said something stupid or if I made it really obvious that I liked him. I don't think I did, though you never know. But even though I am worrying a bit, I mostly just feel very happy about it. I mean, I know asking someone to go for a coffee and talking to them for hours doesn't mean they definitely fancy you. I have done the same with Jane and, much as I like her, I don't want to go out with her. But asking someone for coffee does mean they definitely like you and want to talk to you properly. Which has to be a good thing.

The thing is, though, if he doesn't fancy me (which is perfectly possible, I know), I really, really don't want him to know that I fancy him. It would spoil everything, and I like him so much as a friend (as well as a boy I fancy) that losing his friendship would just make the nothing-romantic-ever-happening thing even worse. So I am trying to make it clear that I like him as a friend without making it obvious that I sometimes sit there imagining what it would be like if he just leaned across the table and kissed me. It is surprisingly tricky. But the thought of him knowing that I liked him and feeling guilty for leading me on – the way he felt about Gemma – is much worse.

Oh, I don't know. Maybe I should just stop thinking about all the bad things that might happen. Maybe I should just let myself be happy for now. Even if nothing ever happens, he is a cool person and I like talking to him. And that might be enough, mightn't it?

SUNDAY ☼

I told Cass about fancying Sam. She called in to my house this morning because she'd left her maths book here on Friday (she realised she'd taken it out of her bag when looking for her phone and then forgot to put it back in again), and she needed it to do her homework. Last night I realised it was kind of stupid to worry about my friends being sorry for me, so as soon as we were up in my room, away from my nosy parents, I told her all. It was actually really good to talk about it at last. Though of course, Cass claims she already had her suspicions.

'I can always tell with you,' she said. 'I was right about John too, remember?'

'Yeah, you went on about it all the time,' I said. 'It was really annoying.'

'You're just annoyed because I know you better than you

know yourself,' said Cass, annoyingly.

Still, she really was very sympathetic towards my lovelorn state. In fact, she was shocked to hear I had thought she might pity me or wouldn't understand what I was going through.

'After all,' she said, 'it's not as if I don't know what it's like to fancy a friend and have no idea whether they like you back, is it? And in my case, I didn't even know if Liz liked girls!'

I felt a bit ashamed that I hadn't thought of that.

'Good point,' I said. 'Sorry. Though of course, I don't know if Sam likes girls either.'

'Oh, I'm pretty sure he does,' said Cass. 'He went out with someone in the Gaeltacht last year and he was really into her.'

I stared at her.

'How on earth do you know that?' I said.

'I have my ways,' said Cass.

'What ways?' I said. A terrible thought struck me. 'You haven't been, like, asking him questions on my behalf, have you?'

Cass looked insulted.

'As if I'd do anything so crude,' she said. 'No, remember the other week when Lucy was going to her cousins' in Rathmines and I was going to Liz's house? We all got the bus together.'

'Oh yeah,' I said.

'Well, Liz said something about her time in Irish college this year, and then she and Lucy started comparing Gaeltacht stories. And somehow they got on to the topic of all the romantic scandal that goes on in Irish college.'

'Scandal?' I said. I didn't like the sound of that.

'Oh, Sam wasn't doing anything scandalous,' said Cass. 'I just mean they were talking about how in Irish college there are always loads of people getting together and lots of who-likes-who and "ooh, is she going out with him?" gossip.'

'Ah, okay,' I said.

'Anyway,' said Cass. 'Lucy said that Sam got together with this girl from Cork called Louisa and he was totally smitten. And so was she. Louisa was smitten with him, I mean. Apparently she was yet another person who assumed Sam and Lucy were an item and Lucy had to basically tell her that Sam liked her, and then they got together at a céilí and it was all very romantic. So yeah, they tried to keep it going when they got home but, after a few months, they realised the long-distance thing was too tough, so it all kind of fizzled out.'

'Whoah,' I said. 'Like me and Paperboy. Sort of.'

'See, you're made for each other!' said Cass. 'You both know what it's like to move on because someone is millions of miles away. Or just in Cork. Anyway, Lucy said he did get over her after a few months, but he was pretty sad for a while. So he is definitely not averse to going out with girls. You have a chance.'

This was very good to hear. Of course, it wouldn't have been good if Lucy had told Cass that Sam was still pining for this Louisa girl, but he clearly isn't. So that's something. And Cass said that she thought it was a very good sign that Sam had asked me to go for coffee with him, so maybe I'm not being ridiculously optimistic about that. She couldn't stay for too long because she told her parents she'd be back nice and early to do lots of studying because they too have been going on about exams. Her parents aren't too bad, though. They're getting her a cool new keyboard stand for her birthday.

Oh God, her birthday! I was so taken up by having hot chocolate with Sam I totally forgot about having to get her a birthday present! I'll have to go into town now. I just hope Mum and Dad will give me some money. I feel so guilty – how could I have put meeting Sam above getting a present for one of my two best friends in the entire world?

Although, actually, I didn't sort out getting extra money yesterday before I went into the Knitting Factory, so technically I forgot about it before I'd even seen Sam. Still, I do feel bad. I will get her something really nice to make up for it (as long as it costs under a tenner – I can't imagine I'll get more than that from my parents. They're not made of money, as they never tire of telling me).

LATER

Oh my God. Something bad has happened. Not to me. But … well, I'll just write it down. I managed to borrow present money off Dad, who gave in to my demands surprisingly quickly. I don't think he was paying too much attention to me because he was lost in the world of Henry Higgins – he was singing 'I've Grown Accustomed To Her Face' when I found him in the kitchen. Anyway, before he could come to his senses and realise he'd just handed me €15 (which was more than I was expecting), I ran off and got the bus into town. I went to the Gutter Bookshop and got Cass a book she's wanted to read for a while, and then I went to get her some gorgeous-smelling shower gel. I think this was a good balance of presents.

Once I'd got Cass's booty, I set off for the bus stop, but as I was approaching a café on Wicklow Street a familiar figure sitting inside it at a table near the window caught my eye. It was Tom! Of course I hadn't seen him since before he dumped

Rachel and broke her heart into a million pieces. Over the last few weeks he's become such a villain in our house it was quite a shock to see him just sitting there looking perfectly normal. I didn't want him to see me because it would be weird and awkward, so I crossed to the other side of the road.

And that was when I noticed he was sitting at the table with a girl. At first, all I could see was her fair hair, but when I walked on a little bit and looked back cautiously I could see her face. And I almost gasped aloud. Because it wasn't just any girl – though any girl would have been bad enough.

It was Jenny.

As soon as I saw it was her I just froze. What was Jenny doing huddled in a café with the boy who broke her best friend's heart? I stepped back into a shop doorway so I could look at the two of them for a moment longer without being totally obvious. They were talking very intensely and at one stage Jenny reached across and gave Tom something and touched his arm. They did not look like two friends having a casual chat. They looked like conspirators. Or people who were having a secret affair behind their best friend and ex-girlfriend's back.

Anyway, I realised I was starting to look suspicious standing there in a shop doorway so I went on to the bus stop, but I was in a sort of daze until I got home. And now I don't know what to do. I had got used to feeling angry with Tom, but Jenny? She has been Rachel's best mate since they were in primary school and I can't imagine Rachel without her. She's like a member of our family. Maybe this is why I feel almost personally betrayed. I think I might be more upset about this than about Tom dumping Rachel. How could Jenny do this? And how can I look her in the face now I know what she's done? How can I look Rachel in the face, for that matter? I don't know if I should tell her or not. Should I? I feel so guilty knowing about it when she has no idea. Imagine if she knew that, say, John had been cheating on me and never told me. I'd hate it. I need to tell her.

LATER

Oh, I can't, it would just kill her. And besides, why should I do Jenny's dirty work for her? She's the one who has stabbed her best friend in the back. Ugh, I feel sick. Luckily, when I came home from town Rachel was doing her homework and then after dinner I did some of my homework and then we all watched TV for a while. So I wasn't actually on my own with

Rachel all evening. But I will have to decide whether to say something eventually.

Oh, how could Jenny do it? How could she?!

MONDAY ☼

I've been trying to behave normally to Rachel, but I can't talk to her without thinking of my terrible secret and how upset she'd be if she knew about it. But that wasn't half as bad as trying to behave normally to Jenny, who of course, as luck would have it, I seemed to meet every five seconds today. It was like she was haunting me. It didn't help that I had to go into the library before class to give back my library books. I was hoping it wouldn't be her day on the desk, but of course there she was.

'Hey, Bex,' she said cheerfully. 'How were the books?'

Normally, I would have chatted to her and told her to read *Code Name Verity*, but I could barely stomach the sight of her so I just said, 'Good. Here you go.'

I turned to go, but Jenny said, 'Rebecca? Are you okay?'

'Fine,' I said. 'See you.'

And I went out because I couldn't bear to look at her a

minute longer. I felt ferocious with rage.

And of course I couldn't talk about it to Cass or Alice because it didn't seem fair that they should know about it when Rachel didn't. So I felt like my feelings were all bottled up. Though it was a relief to be able to talk about liking Sam – I did tell Alice about that. She was typically sensible and Alice-ish about it, which is always strangely comforting.

'Well, he definitely likes hanging out with you,' she said. 'Though of course you know that already. So I would be cautiously optimistic.'

That is what I will be. Not that I have much energy to think about him at the moment, what with worrying about my sister's happiness all the time. It is all very stressful. And to make matters worse, Vanessa is actually going to be interviewed about Kookie on the radio tomorrow morning, on one of the big breakfast shows!

'I couldn't turn them down,' she said. 'I have to give the people what they want.'

It's certainly not what I want, but alas for humanity I seem to be in the minority. I saw loads of first and even some second and third years wearing Kookie badges today. When I first heard Vanessa say they might release her Kookie song as a single I thought it was ludicrous, but now I'm not so sure. If they did, it'd probably become a huge hit and then Vanessa would record a whole album and become an international star.

In fact, what with worrying about Rachel and listening to Vanessa's boasting, Miss Kelly's usual doom-mongering was a welcome relief this afternoon. She was talking about population density and the terrible environmental consequences of urban developments, and it basically made me want to go and live in a field in the middle of nowhere, far away from all polluting things. Which isn't really very practical, especially for band practices. It might be quite helpful for writing, though. At least there wouldn't be any distractions, unlike my own house, where my parents are currently singing 'The Rain in Spain Falls Mainly in the Plain' in very loud voices.

As for Rachel, she's been in her room all evening, though I heard her talking to Jenny the Evil Traitor a while ago. If this goes on for much longer, I'm going to have to tell her what I know. It's not fair. Though what is? It's not fair that Vanessa should go around being rude and snobby and obnoxious to everyone and then still get exactly what she wants. There really is no justice in the world.

LATER

Actually, there is one good thing. My spot has FINALLY started to disappear. I was worried it was never going to go away.

TUESDAY ☾

Well, now I have further proof that the world is unfair: Vanessa's radio interview. We all knew that she was going to be on just before eight o'clock (she mentioned it every five seconds yesterday) and because I am clearly a deranged masochist (or maybe Vanessa has just worn me down?) I couldn't resist listening. Not that I had a choice, really, because we always have that station on the kitchen radio in the mornings.

Anyway, the interview was even worse than I thought it would be, which is saying something. The presenter seemed to love Vanessa. In fact, she introduced her with the words, 'Now, if you've watched any television recently, chances are you'll have seen a new ad with a very catchy tune. The new campaign from Bluebird Bakery features a girl who's, well, a little bit kooky. And it seems like everyone is now singing her song.'

Then they played a snippet of Vanessa singing about having a kooky little day.

'The star of the ad is a Dublin schoolgirl called Vanessa Finn, and she's joined us in the studio,' said the presenter when the song finished. 'Good morning, Vanessa!'

'Hi there,' said Vanessa in a smarmy voice. 'It's great to be here!'

'So, Vanessa,' said the presenter. 'In the ad, you play a character called Kookie, and people have really taken her to their hearts. Tell us a bit about Kookie and why she's so appealing.'

'Well,' said Vanessa. 'She's a teenage girl who likes the quirky things in life. If it's a little bit weird or a little bit fun, then it's totally Kookie!'

I thought I was going to get sick. I had to put down my toast. Rachel pretended to throw up. Even Mum and Dad looked a bit ill.

'And I think that's why people like her so much,' Vanessa continued. 'She's a reminder that we all just want to sing and play!'

Ugh. It was all so sugary it made me want to never smile again, let alone sing or play.

'And what about the song?' said the presenter. 'There are rumours it might be released as a single ...'

'And I'm happy to say those rumours are true!' said Vanessa. "Little Bit Kooky" will be released digitally on Friday.'

Oh for goodness's sake. Vanessa went on to say that some of the proceeds from the single will go to a charity, so I can't actually hope it's a huge flop. But still!

'So what about you, Vanessa?' said the presenter. 'Tell us about yourself.'

'Oh I'm just an ordinary girl,' said Vanessa modestly, which was a reminder that she really is good at acting, as she is probably the least modest person in the country. 'I'm from Glasnevin, and you know what we northsiders are like – salt of the earth!'

Now this is a change! Vanessa used to basically pretend she was from the poshest parts of south Dublin and acted like we, her fellow suburban north Dubliners, were essentially street urchins. Now she has clearly decided to embrace her northside roots. Though she is hardly 'salt of the earth' (neither am I, for that matter, but I'm not on the radio pretending I am). Her dad is an accountant and they live in a very nice Edwardian redbrick house in Glasnevin (which Vanessa used to describe as some sort of palace – it was quite a surprise when I saw it for the first time on my way to Ellie's house back in first year).

Anyway, Vanessa kept going on about how 'ordinary' she

was, which initially baffled me because it was so out of character for her, until I realised she was saying all these things to highlight what a brilliant actress she is!

'My life isn't as colourful as Kookie's,' she said. 'But being able to channel her has allowed me to bring a bit of colour into my life. I think we can all have a kooky little day, every day!'

It truly was sickening. Luckily, the presenter didn't let her ramble on for too long.

'Well, thanks, Vanessa,' she said. 'And I'm sure we'll be hearing a lot more from you in the future!'

Well, I know I will. Unfortunately. It all wouldn't be so bad if it were just a little local station, but it was the biggest station in the country, so thousands, if not millions, of people have heard it while they were having their breakfasts. I just hope some of them saw through Vanessa's sugary act on the programme and realised what a power-crazed egomaniac she is. It makes me wish that episode of *My Big Birthday Bash* had actually been broadcast. If the Irish public had seen her riding around in a giant pink tank like a frilly dictator, they wouldn't be so charmed by her now.

When I got to school, an hour or so later, it seemed like everyone had heard Vanessa's interview. Everyone was talking about it when Cass and I were hanging up our coats in the cloakroom.

'It's so great about the single,' said Karen. 'You never know, maybe it'll lead to a music career.' She noticed me and Cass. 'Sorry, Rebecca,' she said snidely. 'It looks like Vanessa's beaten your little band to glory.'

I took a deep breath and tried to think of how Karen had stood up for Cass during the summer. I could tell Cass was doing the same thing because she just said, 'Well, I don't think we're after the same market.' Then she strolled out of the cloakroom, and I followed.

'Well played, Cass,' I said. 'I knew you wanted to say something ruder than that.'

'I did,' said Cass. 'But sometimes you have to, I dunno. Rise above things.'

'Be noble,' I agreed. 'And I suppose Karen isn't half as bad these days as she was last year.'

'On the other hand,' said Cass, 'Vanessa is even worse. Still, you win some, you lose some.'

This is true. Apparently this weekend Vanessa is going to be doing some promotional events in big shopping centres in her Kookie guise. Imagine going all the way to a shopping centre to gawp at Vanessa. A few weeks ago I would have laughed at the idea that anyone would turn up, but nothing would surprise me now.

Luckily, I didn't have to talk to Jenny today. I just saw her in the corridor near the art rooms, but it was quite crowded so I could easily pretend I hadn't seen her. I can't avoid Rachel forever, though. Our parents are currently at their rehearsal and I've been lurking up in my room doing my homework (and writing in my diary), but *Laurel Canyon* is on soon and I do want to watch it. And if we're both engrossed in telly I won't be tempted to say anything about my terrible secret. Well, really it's Jenny and Tom's terrible secret, but I feel so guilty about knowing it that it might as well be mine.

LATER

Things with Rachel were fine this evening, partly because it was such an exciting and shocking episode of *Laurel Canyon* that it completely distracted both of us. I haven't seen Rachel so animated in weeks. She was even more lively than when Vanessa's ad had its première. Who knew it would take sexy Jack Rosenthal being accused of his best friend's murder to get her all excited? In fact, we were still talking about it (Rachel says there is a chance he might actually have done it, I say no way) in the kitchen when Mum and Dad got home.

'Hi girls!' said Dad, looking very cheerful.

'How was rehearsal?' said Rachel.

'It went pretty well, I think,' said Dad. He picked up an apple that was sitting on the counter and took a bite. 'I think I'm really getting somewhere with Henry Higgins.'

I looked at Mum. She hadn't said anything since she got in.

'How was it for you, Mother dear?' I said.

'Oh, fine,' she said. 'The director's pretty happy with how things are going.'

Rachel and Dad went into the sitting room, but I stayed with Mum in the kitchen.

'Is Henry Higgins really going somewhere?' I said.

Mum looked slightly stressed. 'Well, Laura's happy with it. And it really is very imaginative. But I'm not sure what the rest of the cast think. Tonight he suggested that he should appear as a sort of dancing dream figure when Eliza sings "Wouldn't It Be Loverly".'

'Wow,' I said.

Mum sighed.

'I know some of the cast think he's trying to steal the show,' she said. 'But it's really not that at all. It's just that he loves dancing so much. And he really doesn't get to do enough of it in the usual Henry Higgins part. So he's just trying to find opportunities, and maybe he's finding too many of them ...'

Then she seemed to pull herself together. 'But I'm sure it'll all work out,' she said briskly. 'And your dad is a total professional!'

I am not so sure about that. A dancing dream figure! He has definitely lost the run of himself. If the rest of the cast haven't risen up in protest against him in a week I will be very surprised. But sad too. Poor Dad, why didn't they just give him the part of Alfred in the first place?

WEDNESDAY ✿

In the past I got very bored on the few occasions when Miss Kelly confined herself to the bare facts and didn't bother terrifying us with environmental disasters, but as the exams grow nearer I am genuinely starting to worry about her unique approach. I mean, I'm not a huge fan of geography, but I do want to at least get an honour in it. Today she just talked about climate-fuelled migration and how huge chunks of the earth will be uninhabitable and that we'll be lucky if Dublin isn't under water by the time we're forty. It is all very scary and is definitely making me very conscious of recycling things and unplugging things when they're not being used, but will it be any use in the actual exams?

Also, I'm starting to worry that I am a sociopath because, as the week goes on, it's becoming easier and easier not to say anything to Rachel about what I saw on Saturday. I didn't even think about it all evening. And apart from when I was in the front room doing my homework and she was in her room doing hers, we were around each other most of the time, what with dinner and telly watching and just sitting around talking rubbish with our parents. But eventually Rachel said something about going out with Jenny on Saturday and that reminded me of her so-called friend's behaviour. And then I felt so angry I was sure it would show on my face, so I went off to bed. Well, to my room, where I am writing this.

Oh, why did I have to see them on Saturday? It would be so much easier if I didn't know anything.

THURSDAY ◎

Today is Cass's birthday. She is now fifteen, same as me (Alice won't be fifteen until next month). We're going to have the proper birthday celebration in the Milk Bar, that cool retro place that sells nice burgers and milkshakes and stuff, after practice on Saturday, but at lunchtime today Alice, Ellie, Emma and I presented her with our presents because if you have to go to school on your birthday, you might as well have some presents to cheer you up. I only gave her half of her present so I have something to give her on Saturday. She was delighted.

'I think all birthdays should be spread out over a few days,' she said. 'Much better than getting all the good stuff in one go.'

Ellie had made Cass a really cool birthday card and also gave her a little case for her phone which she had made out of a great fabric with owls on it. It was an excellent present, not least because it's totally unique – no one else will have a phone case like it. This is the good thing about making things rather than buying them. Maybe I should teach myself how to sew? I bet Ellie would teach me; she said her session with Lucy went very well. Although with the sweet-making and the songwriting and the poem and story writing AND the band practising I'm not sure when I'd find the time.

Teachers are not very sympathetic about birthdays. Cass

and I got a tiny bit giddy during history because I passed her a picture of herself as an oppressed peasant being booted out of a cottage by an evil landlord. We were only laughing a little bit but Mrs O'Reilly separated us again, even though I told her it was Cass's birthday and I was just giving her birthday greetings. It was so unfair.

Mrs Harrington, on the other hand, wished Cass a happy birthday when she saw the card from Ellie sticking out of her folder. She isn't so bad, really, especially now she's not going on about Mum's books all the time. I suppose she has enough to think about, writing a book of her own. I wonder if she's heard back from any agents yet? I can't imagine anything will happen, to be honest. I think she's just got her hopes up for nothing.

Speaking of my mother, she and my dad are still at rehearsal. I wonder if the cast has risen up against Dad yet? I am afraid it is only a matter of time now.

LATER

Well, the great *My Fair Lady* uprising hasn't taken place yet, but it's definitely coming. Dad wasn't his usual exuberant self when he and Mum got home from rehearsal.

'How did it go tonight?' asked Rachel.

'Oh, fine,' said Dad. 'But ... I don't know. Everything felt a bit flat. I'm just not feeling the energy from some of the cast.'

'What do you mean?' said Rachel.

'Well, I just had a few ideas, and some of the others weren't really keen,' said Dad. 'I'm not sure they really get what I'm trying to do.'

Oh dear. I bet he was going on about the dancing dream figure.

'What did you think, Mum?' I said, giving her a meaningful look.

'Oh, you know what rehearsals are like,' she said briskly. 'Some go better than others.'

Someone is going to have to talk some sense into Dad before he alienates the entire cast. They are obviously getting annoyed by his suggestions. I thought Mum would say something, but clearly she doesn't want to burst his bubble. So maybe it will be up to me, as I seem to be the only person who knows what needs to be done. I wish I wasn't, though. Sometimes being right about stuff is a heavy burden.

Just realised that because of Cass's birthday bash (ahem) I won't be able to talk for long with Sam after practice on Saturday. Not that he will definitely want to talk to me for ages, of course. Still, I'll be hanging out with some of my best friends in a cool café, so it's not like I'll be suffering. And I'll still get to chat with him for a few minutes in the Knitting Factory. Even a small chat warms my heart. I only get to see him once a week, after all.

FRIDAY ☺

This morning Mum insisted on changing the radio station in the kitchen because there was an interview with a really right-wing campaigner who she can't stand.

'If I have to listen to that man go on about how women are responsible for everything that's wrong in society for one more minute, I'll start throwing plates,' she said, hitting one of the radio's preset buttons. I had no problem with this at all, because I didn't particularly want to listen to him either. But as soon as she switched stations, a horribly familiar voice came out of the radio.

'Oh God, Vanessa's ad,' I said. 'Ugh.'

'It's going on for a bit longer than usual, isn't it?' said Rachel, looking up from her toast. And we realised it wasn't just the ad. It was the single! Three whole minutes of Vanessa going on about how kooky she is. I know we could have just turned the radio to another station, but it was like we were frozen in horror. Unsurprisingly, the extra lyrics were just as bad as the ones we'd already heard in the ad. Poor Handsome Dan even got brought into the whole sorry mess!

> *My dog might be a little bit ugly*
> *But he's my little protegé*
> *And besides, he's totally cuddly*
> *He celebrates each kooky little day*

How unfair! Handsome Dan is not ugly at all; he's lovely. And needless to say, 'cuddly' does not rhyme with 'ugly'. There was an extra middle eight in the song too, as if the normal tune wasn't enough.

> *Life can be fun*
> *When you play in the sun*
> *And just let your kooky flag fly*
> *So join in with me*
> *And together we'll see*
> *That quirky kids can go sky high*

I wish Vanessa would go sky high. In a rocket, and never come down again. Of course, when I got to school it seemed like everyone had heard the song on some station or another. Vanessa managed to reach new heights of smugness, which I actually hadn't thought would be physically possible. But it appears it is.

'It's all for a good cause,' she was saying when we went into Irish, our first class of the day. 'I'm happy to do my bit.'

'What's the charity again?' asked Karen.

Vanessa's face froze for a second.

'It's for children,' she said. 'Like, children who need help.'

And then our teacher came in, so she didn't have to say anything else. I knew she doesn't care about doing her bit for society, but not even knowing the name of the charity is a bit much, even for her. She'd better remember it before she does all her promotional work this weekend. Anyway, I wish the single's proceeds weren't going to a charity, whatever that charity might be. If it was just going to make Vanessa and whoever wrote the song rich, I could wish it would be an enormous flop without feeling guilty at all.

Speaking of feeling guilty, I still keep forgetting about the whole Tom and Jenny thing and then I'm reminded of it and feel awful. I just keep thinking what it'll be like when Rachel finds out and discovers that I knew all about it. She'll be very angry, and rightly so. She'll feel betrayed by me as well as Jenny.

But every time I think about telling her, something happens

and she's sad and I just can't bring myself to do it – like, this evening she went to the cinema with a bunch of her friends from school (not including Jenny – I bet the evil traitor was off with Tom) and when she came home she was all subdued.

'Are you okay?' I said.

'Meh, I dunno,' she said. 'The film was good, but it was all about a couple breaking up and ... ah, it just made me think of the whole Tom mess.'

'Have you talked to him?' I said. 'Since that time you met up.'

'No,' she said. 'We've sent each other a couple of texts and messages. And ...' She looked a bit embarrassed. 'I've kind of checked him out on, um, various social media things. More than once. But I think I should unfriend him and stop looking at anything online. I mean, I dunno. A clean break. You don't get over people otherwise.'

She's right. I know we didn't drop all contact, but I felt much better about the whole Paperboy thing once I stopped expecting contact from him (and being disappointed). It's still sad, though. I tried to remember those 'how to cheer up your dumped friend' tips. The only doable thing I could think of was 'make them laugh'. So I suggested that we have a sitcom box-set binge.

'Okay,' said Rachel. 'I'll make my special hot chocolate.'

Twenty minutes later, we were in front of the telly and she was laughing so much she nearly rolled off the coach. So that tip really did work. And I was having a good time too. It's good having a sister who finds the same things funny as you. I nearly told her about Sam, but I was trying to keep her mind off all things romance-related, so I didn't.

SATURDAY ☺

Very exciting news – we're going to play a gig in three weeks! Veronica turned up when a bunch of us were arriving at the Knitting Factory and told us the news. She has arranged for the Knitting Factory to let us put on an under-eighteens show. We were lucky to get on the bill because only four bands can play this first one – there'll be another one happening next month, though, and hopefully it'll become a monthly thing after that. Anyway, first up are us, the Wicked Ways, Puce and Bad Monkey, which is an excellent line-up. I wonder if Puce have made their stage show even more dramatic since the summer? They did a lot of jumping on top of things and dancing around in front of back-drops – it was very impressive.

Exquisite Corpse and Small Paula, who were all at the Knitting Factory today for the first time in a few weeks, will be playing the second one along with two other bands we don't know. Tall Paula is glad that they got the second gig.

'We've been working on some new songs,' she said, 'and there's no way they'd have been good enough to play live for the first session. But we should be okay for the next one after that.'

Small Paula didn't say much, as usual, but she seemed pleased.

'Have you written lots of new stuff since the summer, Paula?' asked Cass.

'Lots? I don't know,' said Small Paula. 'You'll see.'

She is still very mysterious. I do like her, though. I wish I could be as enigmatic as her. I tried it during the summer, but it just confused people.

Richard and the Wicked Ways are excited about playing the gig too, though Richard is a bit worried that he won't be able to steal his big brother's cool suit, which is what he usually wears to gigs.

'He's hidden it in a new place,' he said. 'I have no idea where it is. It's not at the back of his wardrobe anymore.'

'Well, you've got a few weeks to find it,' said Cass comfortingly. 'Maybe it's up in the attic or something?'

'And if you don't find it,' said Alice, 'you can wear that cool shirt your uncle got you in London, and those black trousers.'

'Yeah, I suppose I can,' said Richard. 'I think the suit's spoiled me, though. Nothing else is as good once you've worn a suit like that.'

'Maybe Ellie could make you one?' I said.

'I know Ellie's very good at clothes-making, but I don't think she's up to suits yet,' said Cass.

'I don't know,' said Alice. 'Those shorts were pretty good.'

'There's a big difference between a pair of shorts and a whole suit,' said Cass. 'Especially as Ellie is a short girl and Richard is a tall boy.'

But Richard looked thoughtful.

'I dunno, she did help Mrs Limond alter all the suits when we were doing the musical,' he said, running a hand through his quiff (which isn't quite as big as it was during the summer, when he seemed to be subconsciously imitating his musical idol Ian Cliff, but is still quite impressive).

'Well, you can ask her later at my big birthday bash,' said Cass. 'After I ride in on my pink pony.'

'Your what?' said Tall Paula. So we had to explain about Vanessa's attempt to be on the telly show.

'And now she's in a stupid ad,' I said. 'For Bluebird Bakery cookies.'

'Oh my God, is she Kookie?' said Tall Paula.

'I'm afraid so,' I said with a sigh.

'Half my class are singing that song,' said Tall Paula. 'Some of them are even dressing like her. Everyone's gone Kookie mad!'

'"Mad" being the perfect word,' said Cass grimly.

'It's a very catchy song, though,' said Tall Paula. 'I mean, it's terrible. But it's catchy.'

'Kooky little day?' said Small Paula. 'Huh!'

And she walked off to her studio.

'That's the best response to Vanessa's ad I've heard yet,' said Cass, admiringly.

Then we all realised we were wasting precious practice-room time, so we went off to our various studios. Our practice went very well. The song with the lyrics about standing up for yourself is now called 'What Tastes Better (Is Honesty)' and it's pretty much finished now – I think we'll be able to do it at the gig. In fact, considering each band's set at the gig will have to be pretty short, we won't be able to fit all our songs into it – we'll have to decide what to leave out. And just think, a year ago we only had one original song to play at the Battle of the Bands! Now we have almost a whole album's worth of songs. If we were going to record an album. Which we might, you never know.

Anyway, after the practice we met Richard and Liz, who were of course coming to Cass's birthday celebrations. Cass had told Ellie we'd meet her outside the Knitting Factory, so we all went out to wait for her – and for Emma and Jane, who were joining us too. After a few minutes, Ellie walked out with Senan and Lucy. My heart rose at the thought of seeing Sam, but alas there was no sign of him.

'No Sam today?' I said, as casually as I could. I avoided Cass's eye as I said it, in case she looked at me in a meaningful way.

'No, he had to leave half an hour early,' said Lucy. 'Daire's taking part in a skateboarding contest thing and Sam promised he'd go and cheer him on.'

'Ah, okay,' I said. I hope I didn't sound as if I was bothered one way or the other. Even though I was really disappointed. I didn't mind about not getting to talk to him for long today, but I did want to just see him and say hello.

'Do you two want to come along to the Milk Bar?' said Cass. 'It's my birthday party. Well, sort of a party. I bet they could fit a couple of extra seats.'

Senan had to go to his brother's football match, but Lucy happily accepted Cass's invitation. Then Emma and Jane arrived, so we all headed over to the Milk Bar, settled into our giant table near the window and ordered a giant and delicious feast (well, some burgers and milkshakes and Coke floats).

'If only we could do this every week,' I said.

'Well, it's my birthday fairly soon,' said Alice. 'So we can have a bit of a celebration then.'

Richard asked Ellie about the suit. She looked thoughtful.

'I definitely couldn't make one from scratch, I'm afraid,' she said. 'It's too complicated. I mean, most tailors train for years.'

Richard looked a bit disappointed.

'Oh well,' he said. 'Maybe in a few years, then.'

'But!' said Ellie. 'I did learn quite a bit about alterations from Mrs Limond. So if you happen to have a suit that isn't as perfect a fit, I could change it a bit.'

'Wow, really?' said Richard. 'Thanks! I have a cheapish one that I had to get for my cousin's wedding back in February. Maybe you could do something with that?'

'Well, I'll give it a try,' said Ellie. 'But I can't promise miracles.'

Jane wanted to know how Vanessa's fame had affected her at school.

'Just as badly as you can imagine,' I said.

'I'm kind of intrigued by Vanessa,' said Liz. 'I've only seen her on stage in *Mary Poppins* and she was pretty good.'

'Just count your blessings you don't have to put up with her off stage,' said Cass, eating a chip.

'Vanessa's mum has basically become her publicist,' said Jane. 'Every time she sees my mother – or me, for that matter – she starts telling us how brilliantly Vanessa is doing and how it's only a matter of time before she's a superstar and what a pity it is that I'm not so committed to my acting career.'

'She sounds just as bad as her daughter,' said Cass.

'Not quite, but almost,' said Jane. 'My mum is getting really sick of it, even though Mrs Finn is her friend. She says when I start putting on plays, she'll go on about it to Mrs Finn all the time, but to be honest I don't think Mrs Finn would be impressed. Oh well.'

Then Ellie said, 'God, look who it is! Outside, over there.'

We all looked where she was pointing.

'Ugh,' I said. 'Charlie!'

It was awful Charlie, the sexist, pervy bully who said horrible things about Cass at the end of the summer camp. He was strutting along the street with Robbie, who had been in his band the Crack Parrots. The band broke up when two of the members walked out because they couldn't bear hanging around with Charlie anymore.

'I think he's noticed us,' said Alice. 'Yes, he definitely has.'

'That's the infamous Charlie?' said Liz. 'Hmmph. Let's just pretend we can't see him.'

'No,' said Cass firmly. 'Let's not. Let's give him a big wave.'

'What?' I said.

'Well, look at us,' said Cass. 'There's a big gang of us, hanging out, having a good time. And he's stuck with Robbie because half his mates ditched him for being so horrible.'

'It's true,' said Richard, who goes to the same school as the Crack Parrots boys. 'He hasn't been the same since the summer. Thank God.'

So, as he went past, we all cried 'Hi, Charlie!' and waved at him with big fake smiles on our faces. Cass put her arm around Liz and kissed her on the cheek. Charlie looked really embarrassed and walked past really quickly, and we all cracked up. In fact, we were laughing so loudly he could probably hear us halfway down the street.

And then Liz brought out a big birthday cake her mum had made for Cass (she checked with the Milk Bar that it was okay to bring our own cake, and they were cool about it). And we all sang happy birthday and everyone in the restaurant joined in. It was a brilliant afternoon. In fact, I didn't think about Sam the whole time. I'm thinking about him a bit now. But mostly I'm remembering how great it was when we all showed Charlie that his stupid bullying had just made us stick together more.

MONDAY ☼

Vanessa was on the front page of the *Irish Independent* today. Seriously. There was a photo of her in a posh southside shopping centre surrounded by gullible members of the public, all dressed as Kookie! What a terrible sight. She is, of course, delighted with herself. She took the paper into school and kept showing it to everyone.

'It was so great to meet my fans,' she said.

'The song was on the radio twice this morning,' said Karen. 'No wonder people are lining up to meet you!'

I couldn't help thinking of how Karen behaved when I accidentally ended up in the paper after Mum's book came out. How things have changed.

On the plus side, I think Alison has totally given up on Karen at last. I hope Alison becomes a super successful tech genius millionaire and leaves both Karen and Vanessa far behind. She spent all of lunch today with Emma talking about this computer course they are both doing. I chatted with them for a while. It sounds pretty interesting, actually. You can do all sorts of impressive things if you learn code, which is basically computer language.

But I don't have time to take on any extra challenges myself. I'm busy enough as it is. It feels like all our teachers were going on about it being an exam year again today. And it's not like I'm not studying. I spent all of yesterday (well, at least an hour) doing my homework! I'm doing my bit! And I've just done tonight's homework, even though the awful Mulligan child popped up at her window and danced at me for a while. Thank God the clocks are going back soon and it'll get dark earlier. She won't be able to taunt me when my bedroom curtains are drawn.

TUESDAY ☾

Had to go to the dentist for a check-up after school today. I live in fear of the dentist even though I have no fillings (yet). I keep feeling that my luck will run out eventually. I also worry that she'll tell me I need to get braces. My teeth look pretty straight, but so did Ellie's last year and then the dentist told her she needed train-tracks to correct her bite. She told him her bite seemed to be working perfectly, but he disagreed. She's used to her braces now, though. And they'll be off in another six months or so. Still, I'm glad I don't have to get any braces (yet. Touch wood). And I was very relieved that my teeth are fine and will stay filling-free for the moment. I ate a Wispa to celebrate, though I'm not sure that's what my dentist would have wanted. I did brush my teeth straight afterwards, though.

Mum and Dad's rehearsal went well tonight. At least, they claim it did. Mum said it's still all 'coming along nicely', but they are both a bit more subdued after rehearsals these days than they were a few weeks ago, presumably because Dad is still pushing his luck with the rest of the cast. On the plus side, Rachel and I had a very civilised evening watching Jack Rosenthal try to get out of jail in *Laurel Canyon*. It was very exciting and it definitely distracted Rachel from her woes.

In fact, though there are still times when she goes to her room and plays sad music and is probably crying, Rachel has been pretty normal this week. It seems like she really is getting a bit better, slowly but surely. Which is why it's so awful about Jenny and Tom. And weirdly, her seeming like her normal self makes it even harder for me to think of telling her the truth than when she was upset – I can't bear the thought of making her miserable again. Ugh, I can't think about it now. I'm going to go and read for a while and think about imaginary people's problems. They generally have a happy ending. Though not always – I've read a few brilliant books lately that made me cry buckets at the end.

WEDNESDAY ❀

Cass, Alice and I are debating whether to put together a stage set for the gig. Cass, unsurprisingly, is in favour.

'It'd be easy!' she said. 'Remember what Puce did at the summer-camp gig. It looked really good and it didn't take much stuff. All we need is a few old sheets and some paint! And maybe a standard lamp or something.'

It's true, Puce's stage set was simple but really impressive.

'But when are we going to find the time to paint sheets?' said Alice. 'We've only got two and half weeks!'

'That's loads of time,' said Cass.

'What if we can't find sheets at all?' I said. 'I think all the old sheets in my house have patterns on them.'

'Stop looking for problems!' said Cass. 'We'll find plain sheets somewhere. Now, what will we paint on them?'

We discussed this for some time. I suggested lots of dolls' faces, but Alice said people mightn't know they were dolls and think they were just random people. She suggested something simple but colourful, like a rainbow. Cass said a rainbow was too boring and she wanted more of a challenge.

'What about a giant version of our band logo?' I said.

'In rainbow colours!' said Alice. 'Like, it can look as if the letters are windows and you can see a rainbow through them.'

'Hmmm,' said Cass. 'That might work. I'll get working on some sketches.'

I think it could look really good. I hope we do have enough time to do it. I know the gig is over two weeks away, but we'll be at school for most of it.

THURSDAY ◎

Oh dear. I knew it was going to happen and it has. Our parents went off as usual to their rehearsal, and Rachel and I were watching telly when, at around half past nine, we heard a sound from the hall.

'Was that the door?' said Rachel.

'It can't have been,' I said. 'I don't hear any singing.'

But a moment later Mum and Dad came in. Mum looked a bit stressed and Dad looked downright miserable.

'Is everything okay?' said Rachel. 'What happened?'

I already knew the answer.

'Ah, the rehearsal didn't go that well,' said Mum.

'It was fine,' said Dad. 'I just ... misjudged a few things. About the part.' He yawned. 'I'm too knackered to talk about it, actually. But it's all fine. Let's just watch some telly.'

But when Dad went to the loo, I asked Mum what really happened.

'It was all a misunderstanding,' she said. 'But ... well, a few of the other cast members had a word with your dad and Laura. They don't think Ed's contributions are really working.'

'So what does that mean?' said Rachel. 'Has he lost the part?'

Mum looked shocked.

'Oh no!' she said. 'Nothing like that. He's just going to have to, well, tone it down a bit. Stick to the scenes where Henry Higgins usually appears.'

'Are they all really annoyed?' I said. I hated the idea of that. Dad does drive me mad, but he's a decent person really, and I know he didn't want to steal anyone else's thunder.

'Oh no, not now,' said Mum. 'They know he means well. Everyone's fine. But they just found it really distracting and … well, they just didn't think it worked. So he's going to have to go back to the usual Henry Higgins.'

I know this is the right thing to do – I mean, just the bit I saw of Dad's jazzed-up version looked completely insane. And I shudder to think what he would have been like leaping around the stage when Eliza Dolittle was trying to sing a song on her own. But it does seem like a shame that he can't get to do some more dancing. It really is what he does best. Well, I suppose he must be quite good at teaching history and writing research papers about it too, considering that's his job, but he definitely seems to have more fun dancing. Poor Dad.

FRIDAY ☺

Today Mrs O'Reilly showed us some examples of the Junior Cert paper. I have to admit it freaked me out a bit. It made the exams and stuff seem even more real. I was so worried about it I didn't even take advantage of the fact that Mrs O'Reilly seems to have forgotten she forbade me and Cass to sit together last week. I could easily have done one of my trademark historical Cass portraits, but I was too busy worrying about whether I'll be able to cram so much historical stuff into my brain by next June.

Mrs O'Reilly did point out that we haven't actually done some of the topics in class yet, so we shouldn't be too freaked out by the fact that some of the questions were on unfamiliar things, but it was still very unsettling. And it's got me worrying again about geography. I mean, we'll be sorted if the exam is all about eating bugs and cities being submerged by giant tidal waves, but what if it isn't? And I'm also worried about German. After all, the thing about languages is you either understand them or you don't. You can waffle a bit in some exam subjects (even geography), but you can't really waffle at all if you don't have any of the right words. Or, even worse, if you don't understand the questions. Right, that's it. I'm going to try and get the others to practise Deutsch with me tomorrow.

Oh, and at lunchtime today I was giving back one of my library books and Jenny was behind the counter. She tried to talk to me, but I basically ignored her (I said 'Hi' but that was about it) and got the other sixth-year girl to check my books. Jenny may think she can walk all over Rachel, but she can't walk all over me.

SATURDAY ☺

Excellent day! First of all, our practice went really well. The new song will definitely be ready to perform at the gig in two weeks. In fact, we've worked out our set and we can play all the songs through perfectly with no mistakes (apart from when Cass hit the wrong note once on the keyboard. Oh, and I nearly came in at the wrong time during 'The Real Me', but I didn't).

Also, we even managed to talk in German – well, sort of German – for five whole minutes. Though Cass was not enthusiastic at first.

'I don't know why you're getting so hung up on this,' she said. 'There are months to the exams.'

'That's why we need to start now!' I said. 'So we don't have to cram at the end. And besides, we should be taking advantage of the fact that our best friend can speak German perfectly.'

'Not totally perfectly,' said Alice. 'I mean, my cousin Florian thinks I have a totally Irish accent.'

'Well, you're a zillion times better than either of us,' I said. 'So come on, let's talk "auf Deutsch"!'

'You're just panicking, Bex,' said Cass. 'In a couple of days you'll forget all about it. And then in a few months you'll probably panic about it again and make us all talk German until the panic wears off. And it'll go on and on.'

She is probably right. That is the sort of thing I do. But still!

'Well, you'll be glad I made you when we both get As in German next summer,' I said.

Cass rolled her eyes. 'What's the German for "okay"?' she asked Alice.

'Um, they usually just say "okay",' said Alice.

'Okay,' said Cass. '*Spielen wir Musik!*'

That means 'let's play music'. So we did. In fact, we were so busy playing and singing we didn't really say much, in German or otherwise, but we did say '*Wo ist das Microphone?*' and stuff like that. Anyway, it made me feel weirdly less panicky about the exams, so that's something.

When our time in the studio was up, we went out to meet the others. Richard and the Wicked Ways were there, and so were Exquisite Corpse and Puce. The Puce boys are full of ideas for their stage set.

'We're going to have stuff projected on the stage,' said Niall. 'It's quite easy if you hook up a laptop. I asked Veronica and they could set it up.'

I could see Cass's eyes light up at the thought of this.

'Are you going to make a special film?' she asked.

'Um, no, not yet,' said Niall. 'We've found something cool online so we're going to use that and hope no one sues us.'

That sounds a bit risky to me, but I can't wait to see how it turns out. Anyway, then we all strolled back to the art space as usual, and I tried not to get my hopes up in case Sam had gone off to another skating contest or had the flu or something. But when we walked into the studio, there he was. He gave me a big grin when he saw me and came straight over.

'Hey, long time no see,' he said.

'How was the ... was it a skating competition?' I said, even though I remembered perfectly well. I didn't want him to think I'd been thinking about his activities since last week. Even though I had.

'It was a skating competition, and it was pretty good – my friend Daire came second,' said Sam. 'I heard I missed an excellent party, though.'

'You did,' I said. And I told him about seeing Charlie. He laughed and said that was the perfect way to treat Charlie. And he should know – like Richard, he's had to go to school with him for the last few years.

'You know Evan and Finn from the Crack Parrots have

started a new band?' said Sam. 'They were thinking of trying to get a practice space here.'

'Really?' I said. 'Hmm.' My initial reaction to the thought of any of the Crack Parrots turning up in our cool space was annoyance. I didn't want to be constantly reminded of how awful they were. But then I thought of how Evan and Finn had stood up to Charlie in the end and left the band. I suppose they aren't too bad really.

Then Richard suggested that we all go to the Flapper Café, which is near the Knitting Factory, quite nice and also, more importantly, quite cheap, and lots of people thought that sounded like a good idea. Including, to my delight, Sam. So a big gang of us headed down there and luckily there was a free table big enough to fit us all. There were so many of us I worried I'd end up stuck about ten people away from Sam, but somehow I ended up sitting next to him, with Liz on my other side.

And it was a really brilliant afternoon. Richard had brought in his wedding suit for Ellie to try altering.

'What do you think?' he said, passing it across the table to her. She took it and held it up to the light of the window.

'Hmm, it should be doable,' she said. 'I can take it in a good bit. It may not look as good as your brother's suit, mind.'

But Richard didn't care.

'It'll still look cool and dramatic,' he said. Which is, of course, very important for someone like Richard who sings about being a pterodactyl and a fool for love (not in the same song). So they decided that after our teas and coffees he and Alice would go over to Ellie's house for a fitting before Alice went back to Richard's house for dinner.

I wasn't talking to Sam totally on my own much because, obviously, there were loads of other people there and we were talking to Liz and Lucy and the other people sitting near us, but it was really cool to hang out again. We all talked for a while about books (he's reading *1984* by George Orwell at the moment, while Liz is loving Rae Earl's *My Mad Fat Diary*). And he and I did get to talk on our own for a bit.

'I'm looking forward to your gig,' he said. 'I mean, you lot have seen all of our art stuff, but we haven't heard what you've been working on.'

'Well, I hope you're not disappointed,' I said. And then I worried that sounded like I was fishing for compliments, so I said, 'I mean, we've practised hard.'

And then Ellie knocked over her water, and we had to move back to avoid being soaked while she mopped it up, and after that we were all talking in a group again. So that was about as deep as our personal conversation got.

But he said he was looking forward to the gig. And he really did look pleased to see me when we walked into the studio. Every time I think of his big grin, I feel all happy inside. I keep reminding myself that he is a nice, friendly sort of person and perhaps he was smiling at everyone else when I wasn't looking. But every so often I let myself think that there is a chance that he might like me back.

SUNDAY ☼

Poor Dad. As if to taunt him over his recent woes, the film of *My Fair Lady* was on telly this afternoon. Rachel and I were flicking through the channels when the announcer said it was about to begin.

'I kind of feel like watching this,' said Rachel. 'Just to remind myself what it's meant to be like.'

'Should we be reminding Dad of *My Fair Lady* at the moment?' I said. 'I mean, he still seems pretty disappointed about having to tone down his dancing.'

'Well, he's in Mum's study correcting essays,' said Rachel. 'If we keep the volume down, he probably won't even notice.'

Rachel seemed in quite a good mood so I didn't want to kick up a fuss. And so we kept watching. I actually wanted to watch it, because it is a very entertaining film (though it's a bit sexist) and the songs and the costumes are great. In fact, all the music is really good. During the opening credits they played a sort of instrumental medley with bits of all the different songs (this is called the overture, as I remember from my musical days), and all of them were so good I found myself wishing the extracts would go on for longer.

It turned out to be a really good afternoon. It was raining outside, but we were snug on the couch watching a cool old film, and it all felt very cosy and nice.

Rachel seemed pretty happy too, but I can't be happy for her because of Jenny and Tom. It's like I know something bad is going to happen, but there's nothing I can do to stop it, because, whether I tell or not, Rachel will find out eventually anyway and will be miserable (and probably angry at me). I'm trying not to think about it, but it keeps creeping back into my head.

I will distract myself by writing a poem about Sam (just a haiku, they're easier because they're shorter).

Ink hands, messy hair
I do like talking to you

But do you like me?

I think it is quite a mysterious poem. Maybe it's easier to be enigmatic on paper. I certainly can't manage it in real life. This evening I was just sitting on the couch thinking big profound thoughts about LIFE and my mother came in and said, 'If you're just going to sit there staring into space, come and help me change some bed sheets.' No one understands me around here.

MONDAY ☺

I don't believe it. Mrs Harrington is clearly a better writer than I thought she'd be. She was in a very good mood in English today, and when the class was finished she called me over and told me that she has heard back from that agent and he wants to represent her! And he thinks that her book has 'huge bestseller' potential!

'So do thank your mammy for me,' she said happily. 'I'd never have written a word if it weren't for her lovely books.'

'I will,' I said. 'Um, congratulations!'

I am quite happy for her, I suppose, as well as surprised. This time last year she drove me mad, but either I've got used to her or she's calmed down. Anyway, if this agent does sell her book to a publisher, she might take a break from teaching to concentrate on writing.

'Though not before I've seen you all through your Junior Cert,' she told me. I suppose that's for the best, seeing as we've already had two English teachers since first year.

And Mrs Harrington was not the only surprising success story of today. As soon as we got back to our classroom for morning break, Vanessa began talking at top volume about her public appearances over the weekend. Apparently poor Handsome Dan was roped in again, the poor little thing. Anyway, she was in full flow when Karen finally got a word in and said, 'You never know, I might be joining you on screen soon. I've got an audition for a mobile-phone ad on Saturday! And Sarah who runs the drama group thinks I've got a pretty good chance.'

'You've got an actual audition?' said Vanessa, sounding very surprised.

Karen looked annoyed for a moment, then she said, 'Yeah, you knew Bernard and I were looking out for them. You said you'd give us some tips!'

'Well, of course I will,' said Vanessa. 'Now, when they give you the script, here's what you should do first.'

Soon she was in her element, acting like an expert. Of course Karen ate up her every word. Still, I don't think Vanessa would be very happy if Karen did actually get an acting job and stole her thunder. Not that I particularly want to see Karen on screen either, of course. But it would almost be worth it if it stopped Vanessa going on about Kookie all the time.

TUESDAY ☾

Cass has produced some excellent sketches for our (possible) backdrop! She went for the 'imagine the letters spelling out Hey Dollface are windows and you can see a rainbow through them' effect. It really does look very cool. The only issue is whether we'll be able to produce this logo perfectly on a sheet. Cass is, of course, totally convinced that we can.

'I've even found a plain white sheet we can use,' she said. 'So there are no excuses.'

'But what about paints?' said Alice.

'We can just use poster paints,' said Cass. 'Nick has loads of them.'

Even annoying little brothers can be useful sometimes. We have agreed to go over to Cass's house on Sunday afternoon to work on it.

'If it was still summer, we could have done it out in the garden,' she said. 'The more space, the better. But the dining-room table will have to do. It won't take long at all once we get started!' She is convinced we'll get the whole thing done in five minutes despite the fact that none of us has ever painted anything on a sheet before. Including Cass, despite her stage set experience. When we were doing *Mary Poppins,* they were painting on canvas and wood, which is a lot stiffer and less likely to get all crumpled up. I suspect we're going to need a spare sheet, but Cass is worryingly confident. She wanted to try putting together some film projections too, but we talked her out of it because it would just take up too much time.

'One step at a time, Cass,' said Alice. 'We can have projections at the next gig.'

I hope my parents actually let me go round to Cass's house on Sunday. There have been a few comments recently about how I keep staying out all day on Saturday during an exam year. But really, the weekends are meant to be about time off! I think I'm studying pretty hard during the week (well, I'm doing all my homework fairly well and surely some knowledge has to be going in). Also, I will tell them that I have been combining studying with music by speaking German during practice. Surely that will convince them.

I'll have to be careful when I ask, though, because Mum is very busy with work this week. She is finishing the editing of her next adult book (the one with the character named after Mrs Harrington) and getting ready for the publication of the next Ruthie book (sigh), so what with that and the musical she's been a bit frazzled over the last few days. If I ask her at the wrong time, she's quite likely to say no without even thinking about it. This morning I asked her if she'd seen my pencil case and she started going on about how I needed to get more organised in an exam year and how my room was a tip, which is a bit unfair because her study is so messy it looks like the aftermath of an explosion in a book factory.

And Dad wasn't his usual cheery self this evening when he and Mum came home from practice. He clearly feels embarrassed about everyone thinking he was trying to steal their thunder. If only Henry Higgins's songs were a bit more dancy. Or if only there was a part of the show where he could dance without taking all the attention away from the people who were singing.

Oh my God.

There is! I've just had my best idea ever. I must tell Dad straight away.

LATER

I told Dad my genius idea, and he likes it! When I went down-stairs, he was sitting at the kitchen table with a cup of tea and the newspaper in front of him, staring into space.

'Dad?' I said. 'Are you okay?'

'Oh, sorry, love, I was miles away,' he said, smiling at me. 'What's up?'

'Well, I've had an idea,' I said. 'For you and *My Fair Lady*. I know how you can do more dancing.'

Dad sighed.

'I don't think that production needs any more new ideas, I'm afraid,' he said. 'Henry Higgins is just going to stick to his own scenes from now on. The rest of the cast were right, it wasn't fair to them. I don't really know what I was thinking ...'

'No, listen,' I said. 'I don't want you to dance in other people's scenes. I think you should dance in the overture. I mean, to the overture.'

Dad stared at me.

'The what?' he said.

'The sort of instrumental medley of all the songs,' I said.

'I know what it is,' said Dad. 'But what do you mean?'

'Well, before the main part of the show starts,' I said. 'They could play the overture and you could work out a routine for it. You could take all that dancing you added to the getting-married song and 'Wouldn't It Be Loverly', and all that, and put the routines together. Then you'd get to dance AND you wouldn't be treading on anyone else's toes. Not literally. You know what I mean.'

Dad looked thoughtful. Then his face brightened up. 'You know what, Rebecca, that just might work ...' he said. 'It really might. I'll talk to Laura about it on Thursday. Thanks, love!'

He gave me a hug.

'Don't mention it,' I said grandly, and I left him putting on the *My Fair Lady* soundtrack, clearly planning what routine he can do to the overture. At last, I have actually managed to help one of my family (I know I was trying to help Rachel, but I think the whole 'keeping a secret from her' bit might cancel that out)! I just hope Laura the director likes the idea too.

WEDNESDAY ❧

There was another big surprise at school today. And for once, it was a good one! When we arrived for our geography class Miss Kelly strode in and announced that today we were going to run through some sample exam papers (other teachers would probably have just handed them out, but Miss Kelly likes announcing things). As soon as I heard these words, my heart sank. I know we have to see the papers, but I was freaked out enough last week by Mrs O'Reilly, and in her case I was sure we'd actually been spending all our time on the actual subject. So I was almost scared of what I'd see on the geography paper.

And of course, as soon as it landed on my desk, I scanned down the questions and started to feel panicky. I was totally sure we hadn't covered any of these topics. Like urban population growth in India – when had we sat down and studied that? Never, as far as I could tell.

But then something happened. I remembered the times when Miss Kelly went on about how we'd all have to eat bugs because the population of the earth was expanding too fast for us to continue eating the way we've always eaten. As well as the disgusting insect-eating bits, she actually did tell us a lot about population growth and urban development. And then I looked at the question about drawing graphs and remembered Miss Kelly using a similar method to tell us about weather fluctuations. It turns out we have actually been learning lots of geography without really realising it!

I was so amazed by this revelation, I actually said, 'But we've covered loads of this!' out loud in a surprised voice. As soon as I said it, I was horrified. But Miss Kelly looked at me and grinned.

'Of course we have, girls!' she said. 'I'm an educator as well as an environmentalist.'

Who knew you could teach girls so much about geography through the medium of natural-disaster-based terror? It's amazing. I feel much better about the exams now.

I do feel a bit weird about other stuff, though. Well, about Sam. I only get to see him once a week and it's not like we ever text or message each other or have any online contact during the week. What if it's a case of 'out of sight, out of mind'? He might forget all about me as soon as he goes home on Saturday. And I'm worried I've been a bit gushy and overly enthusiastic recently. If he doesn't fancy me (and I must remind myself there is a perfectly good chance that he just sees me as a friend, like Lucy), then I really don't want him to know that I like him. Maybe I will keep my distance a bit this weekend. Well, no, I'm not going to do that. But I will make sure I don't look like I'm totally after him. I will try and get a perfect balance. Oh, fancying someone is all very stressful sometimes.

I was talking about this to Cass on the way home from

school today. She was very understanding, which in fairness to her she has been ever since I told her about liking Sam.

'It's really hard to balance it,' she said. 'I mean, you want them to know you don't hate them, but you don't want them to think you're, like, obsessed with them. Especially if they don't like you back.'

'Exactly!' I said. I sighed. 'I almost wish he wasn't so nice to everyone. I mean, then I'd know he definitely meant it when he was so nice to me. He just seems to like everyone.'

'Well, he doesn't spend ages talking on his own to, say, Ellie, even though he likes her,' pointed out Cass. 'And he hasn't asked anyone else to go and have coffee after the Knitting Factory.'

'That's true,' I said, feeling hopeful. 'That does have to mean something, doesn't it?'

'It definitely means he likes hanging out with you more than most of us,' said Cass.

'Am I thinking too much about this?' I said.

'Meh, not really,' said Cass. 'I mean, before me and Liz got together, I spent an entire week analysing what she meant when she said "I'll see you next Saturday." And I felt I couldn't even tell you or Alice about it, because you didn't know I even liked girls at all and I didn't know what you'd say.'

Poor Cass. Though at least she doesn't have to hide anything now.

'Sometimes it's kind of exhausting doing all that analysing,' I said. 'But once I start I can't really stop.'

'You need to do something nice and distracting,' said Cass. 'Like painting a giant band logo on a sheet.'

'I haven't asked Mum and Dad if it's okay to call over on Sunday yet,' I said. 'They've been on at me about studying again.'

'Just tell them how sorted you are for geography now,' suggested Cass, which is quite a good idea. If I can convince them that I'm on top of my studying, they'll have to allow me some more freedom. I will give it a try.

THURSDAY ◎

Laura likes the idea of an overture dance! I must admit I was quite nervous when Dad and Mum went to rehearsal this evening. If she had ruled it out, he really would have felt miserable. And it didn't help my nerves that Vanessa's ad was shown twice in the space of about half an hour tonight. I didn't think that was legal. Although straight after one of Vanessa's airings, there was a new ad that was genuinely cool. It was for a new national dog-run scheme called Dogtown (they're basically fencing off bits of park so dogs can run around off their leads in them), and it began with a really good hip-hop tune with a cool heavy bassline. Then, one by one, all these dogs walked out of their gardens in time to the music and joined a line of other dogs and kept sort of grooving along slowly down the street until they eventually got to the dog park.

They were real dogs, not animated ones, and I don't know HOW they did it without it looking all cheesy and without CGI, but it looked awesome. I think Handsome Dan might have been in it, but it was hard to tell – I must admit that most pugs do look quite alike. But whoever the dogs were, it was cool and funny. We need more ads like that, not ones with Vanessa showing off!

Anyway, that ad was only a momentary distraction because we soon noticed that it was after half nine and there was no sign of Mum and Dad.

'Do you think Dad's being fired?' I said.

'They wouldn't do that just because he had an idea!' said Rachel, but she didn't look totally convinced. So when the front door finally opened and we heard the two of them singing 'Just You Wait, Henry Higgins', Rachel and I both breathed a sigh of relief.

'Your idea was a hit, Bex!' said Dad, bounding into the sitting room. 'Laura said that if I can work out something suitable, it'll be a really strong opening to the show.'

'And the rest of the cast like it, too,' said Mum. She looked pretty relieved herself. 'He's just got to come up with the choreography.'

'So thanks a million,' said Dad. 'You can be my manager when I leave the dull world of academia and take to the stage.'

'You're not really going to do that, are you?' said Rachel, sounding worried.

'You never know,' said Dad, but he winked at Mum so I knew he was joking. Actually, I think his showbiz fever may have died down a bit when he realised he'd gone too far with his Henry Higgins mania. Now he just has to put together a routine that pleases Laura, but I bet he can. I mean, his moves in that scene I saw were genuinely pretty good, it was just the fact that he was doing them in the background while other people were singing and dancing. So if he does them on his own, I'm sure Laura will like it.

Anyway, he and Mum were in such a good mood I mentioned quite casually that I was thinking of going to Cass's house on Sunday (I told them how well I'd been doing at

247

geography, as Cass suggested) and they are fine about it. Hurrah! Now I just hope this whole sheet-painting thing is as easy as Cass seems to be convinced it is.

FRIDAY ☺

Karen has her audition tomorrow. Vanessa decided to spend lunch today 'coaching' her, which basically involved showing off even more than usual.

Every so often she'd mention the public appearances she did last weekend, or how well the single has done.

'It's still at number twenty-five in the charts this week,' she said. 'I'm so pleased for the charity.'

I bet she still couldn't tell me what charity it is.

'There's no singing in the ad I'm going for,' said Karen (who can, I have to admit, actually sing quite well). 'I wish there was.'

'Well, not every ad offers such a good role as Kookie,' said Vanessa smugly. 'Now, here's how you should enter the room. Shoulders back ...'

But although she was supposedly helping Karen, she kept saying things like, 'You shouldn't get your hopes up too much, anything can happen at an audition.' If Karen actually gets the ad, she'll be furious.

Speaking of ads, I've still got the song from that Dogtown ad stuck in my head. But I don't mind, because it actually is really good. Unlike another ad song I could mention. And unlike the Kookie ad, I don't mind being reminded by the song of all those dogs marching down the street because I liked them. I think I'm going to have to download it; it really is a great song. And maybe playing it will drown out the sound of the *My Fair Lady* overture which is currently blasting through my house. Mum has gone round to Maria's house and Dad is working on some 'moves' in the kitchen, even though there is not much room. He's pushed the kitchen table back against the wall to create a 'studio atmosphere'.

'I told Laura I'd have something for her next Thursday,' he said when I tried to get to the kitchen without him leaping in front of me. I do have faith in his ability to put together a routine, but I wish he could do it somewhere else. Between the thudding and the music it's giving me a headache, and I've got to be fresh and fit for our big practice tomorrow.

SATURDAY ☺

Ellie has done an amazing job with Richard's suit! Seriously, she is a sewing genius. Last week it looked like the kind of baggy suit a teenage boy would be given to wear at a wedding – which indeed it was. And now it looks like something from a cool 1960s film. As soon as we'd finished our practices, we went back to the art space and Ellie handed it over.

'If it's not quite right, I can do some more alterations,' she said. Richard went off to the loo to try it on and when he came back we all gasped, even Sam who admits he doesn't really care much about clothes.

'I don't know how you did it,' said Richard, gazing at his reflection in the glass door (there aren't any actual mirrors in the art space). 'You're a miracle worker.'

'You're a fashion genius!' said Alice.

'Oh, it wasn't that hard,' said Ellie, going a bit red. 'I mean, I didn't make it from scratch.'

And that wasn't the only good thing that happened today. Not only did our practice go very well (though just to be on the safe side we've decided to have one last one before the gig, so we're going to Alice's house after school on Friday, where we can run through the whole set list a few more times), but things were really good with me and Sam. After we'd all been wowed by Richard's new suit, Sam came over to me and said, 'Can I get your opinion on something?'

'Um, sure,' I said. 'What is it?'

'It's the comic I'm working on,' he said, as I followed him across the room to the drawing boards. 'I want an unbiased eye I can trust. Ellie and Lucy don't count – not that I can't trust them, but we've all been working on stuff in the same place for so long that they're a bit too familiar with what I'm doing. Especially Lucy. So basically, I'd love it if you could have a look over this and tell me what you think.'

He picked up his portfolio, which was propped up against the desk, and took out some sheets of paper.

'Here you go,' he said nervously. 'Be honest. But, um, not too honest if you totally hate it.'

I put the sheets of paper on the drawing board and started to read. The story was great – it was a funny, slightly spooky story about a band who sell their souls to the devil to become rich and famous, and then one of them decides to get their souls back.

But what really blew me away was the fact that the pictures were amazing – they were really comic-ish, but they're not, like, cute like Japanese comics. The people look like real people. They were a bit like the ones he showed me by Jaime Hernandez, but they still looked totally original, and there were these amazing, vivid splashes of colour. I'd never seen anything like it. And the pictures went so well with the story.

'Wow, Sam, that's amazing!' I said, forgetting to sound distant. 'I love it!'

'Seriously?' said Sam, looking very relieved. 'Do you think the funny stuff works? I was worried it wasn't quite the right tone ...'

'No, I think it works really well,' I said, and I meant it. 'You could do even more funny stuff with that character Folly. She's great. You could make her even more into the whole selling-her-soul thing. Mike too.'

'Yeah,' said Sam. 'That's a really good idea. But you think it's generally going in the right direction? And the story makes sense?'

'It makes total sense,' I assured him.

'Cool,' said Sam, looking happy. 'Thanks a million, Bex.'

'No worries,' I said, but I felt happy. I do like knowing that he trusts my comics judgement. That has to be a good thing, doesn't it? I just hope I wasn't too gushing. I want to be friendly, yet not too scarily friendly.

We went back to the others and talked about the gig next week. Richard is particularly looking forward to it now he knows he has such an excellent suit to wear.

'I hate to say it, because he did my head in sometimes,' he said. 'But Shane Driscoll was right when he said that the perfect stage outfit can make a difference.'

'Please don't start wearing leather trousers,' said Alice in a worried voice.

Shane was very fond of what he called his 'leather trews'. But there is no danger of Richard adopting the Invited look.

Right, I'd better go and do my homework now so my parents have no excuse to give out to me when I go to Cass's tomorrow. I really don't think they appreciate how hard-working I am.

SUNDAY ☼

Well, we have made a stage backdrop, though, as I thought, it wasn't as easy as Cass kept claiming it would be. For one, we had to weigh down the sheet on the McDermotts' big dining-room table (extended to make it as big as possible) with piles of books in order to make the sheet flat, and that took ages because we kept knocking off the books and accidentally shifting the sheet around. And, once we'd finally got it flat, it was quite difficult for Cass to draw the Hey Dollface logo so that it'd be large enough for people in the audience to see. And THEN we had to figure out where all the rainbow stripey bits should go. It took ages.

But, in fairness to Cass, we did get it done in the end. And it was quite fun once we figured out how to do it properly without making a giant mess. In fact, after a while we got into it and it was almost soothing, just leaning over the table painting away. Alice said she and Richard are thinking about doing some music together.

'Just music that wouldn't be right for either the Wicked Ways or Hey Dollface,' she said. 'It wouldn't be taking away anything from either band.'

'Liz and I keep talking about that too,' said Cass. 'A sort of dancy, keyboardy thing. Probably instrumental. We really need to get round to it. Though as I've told you before, it wouldn't take up any Hey Dollface time. This band is my priority.'

'I'm the only person who doesn't have a musical collaborator,' I said, feeling rather sorry for myself.

'But you've got your writing stuff,' said Alice. 'It's better to do that solo. I mean, most great authors don't have a writing partner, but lots of musical people do. Some creative things are probably better when they're done by one person.'

'True,' I said.

'And you never know,' said Cass. 'If you felt like it, you could always do something with Sam. I mean, you could do a comic, or something.'

I have actually thought about that. I think it would be really good, and not just because of liking Sam as a person. I love his pictures too.

'I haven't been going on about Sam too much recently, have I?' I said. I couldn't help thinking of the days earlier this year when I went on and on about Paperboy all the time and ignored my friends' problems.

'God, not at all,' said Cass, surprised. 'Don't be silly.'

Alice looked guilty.

'You're not still thinking about what I said back in February, are you?' she said. 'Oh no, I feel terrible! It was just that you'd got all wrapped up in Paperboy. You know I didn't mean that you should never talk about yourself again!'

'Fat chance of that happening,' said Cass, but she was laughing so I just poked her with a paintbrush.

'Nah, you were right, I said. 'I was ignoring everyone else.

But I suppose it has made me a bit paranoid.'

'Well, don't be,' said Alice. 'We're your friends. You can talk about whatever you like to us.'

It was a nice afternoon, until I got home where my parents were in full nagging mode. 'I can't remember the last time you did any housework,' said Mum, sending me off to the bathroom with a bottle of Cif and a scrubbing sponge. Clearly she has forgotten all about making me change the sheets of every bed in the house last week. And Dad said I could help him chop vegetables for dinner once I'd finished cleaning the bath. One minute they want me to spend all my time studying, the next they want me to be their household slave. They won't be happy until I have absolutely no free time at all!

MONDAY ☼

Today, after Irish, I ended up walking back to our classroom for lunch with Ellie, and we were passing the library when she said, 'So, what's the story with you and Sam?'

I could feel my face growing hot, but I tried to sound as normal as possible when I said, 'What do you mean?'

'Well, you've been having lots of friendly chats recently!'

she said. 'And ... I dunno, I just thought something was up. There's definitely chemistry between you.'

For a second I thought of saying something. After all, she is my friend, and she has got pretty friendly with Sam and Lucy, and she might know something about what he thinks about me. But then, the fact that she's close to them might mean she'll end up telling them that I like him. And as far as I'm concerned, the fewer people who know about that, the better. So I just said, 'Oh no, there's nothing going on. He's just really sound.'

'Yeah,' said Ellie, who didn't look like she suspected anything. 'He's lovely. So's Lucy. And Senan. In fact, the whole art gang are great. I'm so glad the summer-camp people set up this Saturday thing.'

So am I, and not just because of the Sam thing. Or even because of our practice space, though that is the biggest part of it. But I also love having this place where loads of us who are into music and art and stuff can just ... hang out.

And I know it doesn't really mean anything, but someone else noticing how well me and Sam get on makes me very happy. It makes me feel like I'm not totally delusional for liking him so much. And I really, really do. Like him, I mean.

On a very different note, Karen's audition apparently went

very well. In fact, she's been called back for another audition this weekend. First Vanessa, now her! What is it with my class? It's like St Dominic's is turning into one of those schools on telly shows where everyone's, like, a film star or a pop singer or something. Anyway, Karen was so pleased with how it went she couldn't resist having a few jibes at me, Cass and Alice. It was like old times.

'So another classmate beats you to the spotlight,' she said patronisingly. 'Never mind, I'm sure that band of yours will do something some day.'

'Yeah, probably,' said Cass. 'So did they actually offer you that ad job or not?'

Karen tossed her hair in a move she's clearly learned from Vanessa.

'I'm down to the last four,' she said snootily.

'So they haven't offered it to you,' said Cass. 'Oh well. Good luck and all that.'

Vanessa, unsurprisingly, seems to have mixed feelings about her protegée's success (well, possible success). It's like Karen copying her wasn't so bad when it just gave her an opportunity to be bossy and patronising, but now something might actually come of it she is even less enthusiastic. And it probably doesn't help that Kookie mania seems to be dying down. In fact, there's definitely more of a buzz about the Dogtown ad. I heard the song from the ad on the radio twice today and I didn't hear Vanessa's song once.

TUESDAY ☾

I had a very nice conversation with Rachel this evening when Mum and Dad were out at rehearsal. We had just watched this week's very exciting episode of *Laurel Canyon* (which made me think Rachel is right about Jack Rosenthal actually being responsible for his friend's murder, but only by accident) and Rachel seemed so cheerful and relaxed that, without thinking, I said, 'Rach, you ... seem a bit better this week. About everything.'

'Oh,' said Rachel. 'Well ... I dunno. I suppose I am.'

'Really?' I said.

'Well, not totally better, obviously,' she said. 'I mean, I'm still sadder about it than anything in my entire life. But I suppose I've reached the stage where I'm not actually thinking about it every second. Like, I can forget about it and do normal stuff. For a while, anyway.' And then she looked at me and said, 'You know, I do appreciate you trying to cheer me up. I did notice what you were doing. Even if I didn't show it much.'

'That's okay,' I said, feeling a bit embarrassed.

And then Mum and Dad came in, singing as usual, so our moment of sisterly bonding was over. But I'm very glad all my hard labour was appreciated. And I really am glad she's feeling a bit more normal – some of the time, anyway. I just wish I didn't have the Tom and Jenny stuff in the back of my mind. I manage not to think about it most of the time I'm with Rachel, but whenever I remember I feel guilty and sick.

On a more positive note, I was definitely right about there being more buzz about that Dogtown ad. They keep playing the song on the radio. Even Dad was humming the chorus when he was making the toast this morning. It really is very catchy. And it has definitely taken attention away from Vanessa. There haven't been half as many first years coming in to stare at her or get her autograph over the last few days. In fact, now I come to think of it, I haven't seen half as many Kookie badges this week either. There was a stage when it seemed like half the school were wearing the stupid things. But I did hear two girls humming the Dogtown ad music in the loo this afternoon. Does this mean change is on the way?

WEDNESDAY ❦

Dad has been working very hard on his overture dance all week. He has been practising between lectures in the college gym.

'In front of the students?' I said. I can't imagine it would help you learn about early modern Europe if you'd seen your lecturer dancing around in a tracksuit half an hour earlier.

'Well, there's a sort of studio where classes are held,' said Dad, not looking at all embarrassed. 'So it's not like I'm in the middle of the gym or in front of the climbing wall. But yeah, I suppose some students walk by. I think they like it.'

The mind reels. Though I suppose he really is a good dancer, so it's not like he's totally humiliating himself. Maybe the students are actually impressed. Rachel isn't very impressed by the idea, though.

'Unless something terrible happens at the exams, I'll be going to that college next year,' she said. 'I don't want everyone to know my dad is the lecturer who was gyrating all over the place.'

'Well, you're not going to do history, are you?' I said. 'So it's not like you'll be taught by him. And, besides, no one in your year will have seen him dancing around the gym because they'll all be new, like you.'

'These stories get passed down,' said Rachel grimly. 'People still talk about how Mrs O'Reilly drank half a bottle of champagne thinking it was a fizzy cordial on a school tour to Paris, and then sang "Suspicious Minds" on the bus.'

'Do they really?' I said in surprise. 'I've never heard that story!'

'Oh,' said Rachel. 'Well, they talked about it for years, anyway. I bet the history students won't forget about Dad.' But she looked a bit comforted at the idea that these tales don't last all that long. I think as long as she doesn't do history in Dad's college it'll be fine.

THURSDAY ◉

Oh, what an excellent day. When I was looking at my parents' newspapers this morning there was an article about the Dogtown ad and what makes an ad campaign really take off, and it mentioned Vanessa's Kookie ad, but not in a good way. 'But the Bluebird Bakery campaign has already been forgotten in favour of the new parading pups,' wrote the journalist.

'Because that's the thing about viral media – it moves as fast as, well, a virus. And what was popular one minute is gone the next, replaced by a new feverish cultural fad. While Blue-bird Bakery's Kookie campaign sparked a brief craze here in Ireland, the Dogtown ad has now been viewed by hundreds of thousands of people all over the world, making it the most talked-about Irish-made ad of all time.'

It's become an internet sensation! Apparently people every-where have been going on dog walks and filming themselves and their dogs grooving along the streets to the sound of the ad music. Some people have even done it with dog puppets!

I doubt anyone's ever made a puppet of Vanessa. Unless it was a voodoo doll or something. And the article said there was footage online from Sydney and San Francisco. I don't think Vanessa's fanbase went further than Galway. And I haven't heard the Kookie song once on the radio all week.

In fact, I really think her reign of media terror might actu-ally be ending. There wasn't a single first year sticking her head through the door of our classroom today. I would like to shake the paws of each of the Dogtown dogs to say thank you.

'Well, that's how things go,' said Mum, when I showed her the article this afternoon. 'Things are popular one day and then the next, something new comes along and grabs everyone's attention.'

Speaking of strange cultural fevers, Dad is currently off at rehearsal, showing his dance to Laura and the cast. I really, really hope it goes well. He's put so much work into it. And from the steps he's showed us (he can't do the entire thing at home because there isn't enough room for all his leaping, even if you move the furniture against the walls), it really is quite impressive. But I know there's always a chance she'll decide it's not right. I will just cross my fingers and hope.

LATER

His dance was a hit! I'm so relieved. I was a bit worried all evening in case it went horribly wrong and Laura decided it wasn't going to work. Rachel was worried too.

'I know he's been a bit ridiculous about all this,' she said, 'but he really loves being in that musical.'

When we heard the car pull up, we both looked at each other. Rachel crossed her fingers and so did I.

But as soon as the door opened, we knew things had gone well. Dad was singing 'I'm Getting Married in the Morning', and he positively danced into the room.

'They loved it!' he said, beaming from ear to ear.

'They really did,' said Mum, beaming too. 'In fact, Joe came up and said he understood exactly why Dad had been so keen to let loose his dancing skills.'

'And Laura said it was a perfect way to get the audience in the mood for the show,' said Dad. And he did a little tap dance.

I am very pleased for him. In fact, if it weren't for the ongoing Jenny and Tom secret thing, I would be in a very, very good mood today. I have a weirdly good feeling about Saturday. I don't know why. I just feel like something exciting is going to happen. Something with Sam. Maybe it's because the last time we played a gig at the Knitting Factory, Paperboy kissed me at the end of it. Of course, the last time we played a gig at the Knitting Factory, I also fell backwards off a drum platform and looked completely ridiculous in front of several hundred people. But I'm sure that's not going to happen again. I'm going to check the drum stool very carefully before I sit down, anyway.

And really, maybe it's just that I think if anything is ever going to happen with Sam, surely it will happen at something like a gig, which is basically a party. It seems like the right sort of place. I mean, surely it's more likely to happen there than in the art studio or at the bus stop. Of course, I do know that maybe nothing will ever happen with Sam. And I'm pretty much prepared for that. But IF it does, I really do think it might happen on Saturday. I just have a feeling.

FRIDAY ☺

Today got off to an excellent start because the woman who runs that Li'l Tykes animal performers' agency was on the radio this morning talking about the Dogtown ad – she was one of the animal trainers who worked on it.

'We know they say when it comes to showbiz, you should never work with children or animals,' said the presenter. 'So how do you find working with your canine team?'

'They're an absolute dream,' said the Li'l Tykes lady. 'I've worked with human performers who were much more difficult!'

And I totally know she meant Vanessa, especially because the next thing she said was, 'And the animals like working together too. One of my dogs, Handsome Dan, recently starred in the famous Bluebird Bakery advert, but I think he found this shoot even easier. He had a great time with the other dogs.'

So it really was Handsome Dan in the Dogtown ad! I knew I recognised his adorable squashy features.

Anyway, I don't know whether the radio interview had anything to do with it, but today was the first day in weeks that Vanessa didn't go on about Kookie all the time. She wasn't even wearing the Kookie badge which has adorned her school jumper ever since the ad came out. In fact, I've just remembered that when the campaign started, she said that they were going to make more Kookie ads in the future, but we haven't heard anything about that recently so maybe this is the end of Kookie forever? What a blessed relief. Unfortunately, she had more news for us.

'I've got an audition for a television series tomorrow,' she declared. 'It's a really interesting part. Much more challenging than the Kookie ad. I think it'll really stretch my skills as an actor.'

'If I do get that ad, we can run through our scripts together,' said Karen. 'Help train each other. Bernard and I find that very useful. We can spur each other on.'

I thought Vanessa would be outraged at the idea that she might learn something from Karen, considering how she's been spouting her supposed wisdom at her for weeks, but to my amazement, she said, 'Hmmm, yeah, I suppose we could.'

Maybe finding out that one ad doesn't mean you'll be a big star forever is actually making her more humble and maybe even human? Though I won't hold my breath. She'll probably be lording it over her so-called friends again next week.

Cass and I went to Alice's after school for our last-minute practice. Our parents let us do this on the condition that after this weekend we will knuckle down and concentrate on our studies for a while.

'You spend half the day in town on Saturdays just for your band practices, anyway,' said Mum. 'So that should be enough music and weekend socialising for you. It's back to work on Monday, okay?'

I hope she will forget about this after a while. Seriously, the odd Sunday afternoon out isn't going to make me fail my exams. But I won't argue with her for the moment.

Anyway, the practice went very well (I dropped my drum sticks once, and Alice got a chorus and middle eight mixed up, but we agreed it was just pre-show jitters and that we'll be okay tomorrow). When it was over and we were waiting for Cass's mum to collect her and me and bring us back to

Dublin, we sat around for a while drinking Cokes and talking about stuff.

'I think we should drink a toast to the Dogtown dogs,' said Cass, raising her can of Coke. 'They have taken the country's attention away from Vanessa, and so they have performed a great service to humankind.'

'I'll drink to that,' I said, clinking my can against Cass's. Alice leaned over and clinked her can too.

'Though she might get that TV series,' she said. 'And then she'd be on telly for ages. And it'll probably be even more high profile.'

'Meh, even if she gets it, it won't be on TV for months and months,' said Cass. 'So we'll have a nice break from her nonsense until then.'

'I think we should think about recording something soon,' I said. 'I mean, we learned a fair bit about the technical stuff at the summer camp. And we could get some studio time at the Knitting Factory.'

'Don't you think we should wait until after the exams?' said Alice.

'Oh, we can fit something in before then!' said Cass. 'What about the Christmas holidays? You're not going to spend every second studying then, are you?'

'I suppose not,' said Alice.

'There you go,' said Cass. 'We can record a mini-album then.'

And we probably will. It's hard to believe Cass used to be so nervous about band stuff. She's the most confident of us all these days.

Anyway, I am fairly confident about tomorrow. And very excited. I love playing live so much, even though I've only done it twice. And Kitty will be there to see how we've come on since she last saw us on stage. And so will Sam. And I really, really hope something will happen with him. Surely something will? I can't feel so butterflies-in-my-tummy-ish for nothing.

LATER

I just went downstairs to find Jenny the Traitor lolling about in my sitting room with Rachel. I don't know how she dares show her face in this house after what she's been doing. And it turns out she is staying the night! She is truly shameless. I'll try to avoid her as much as possible. It shouldn't be too hard as I want to practise my drums a bit more in preparation for tomorrow. I've just spent twenty minutes playing along on my snare to our recording of 'The Real Me'. I think I've actually got better at drumming since we recorded it – when I listen to it I keep thinking of things I'd do slightly differently now. So I'll just think about drumming and tomorrow's gig and not about the evil traitor in my house.

SATURDAY ☺

It's only eleven o'clock, so I don't have to leave the house for ages, but I can't bear to go downstairs because Jenny is still here. My parents have gone to the garden centre yet again to buy some new winter shrubs, whatever they are, and Rachel and Jenny are in the kitchen drinking mugs of Rachel's special hot chocolate, which she only makes for special occasions and which Jenny definitely does not deserve. Just the thought of her sitting there drinking that delicious treat is sending me into a rage again. How can I just sit here when I know what she's done?

Oh, screw this, I can't. I can't let her fool Rachel a second longer. It's gone on for too long. I'm going to do what I should have done weeks ago. I'm going to go down and confront her. It has to be done.

Right. Here I go.

LATER

Oh God. I have made a big mistake. A really, really stupid mistake. I feel ridiculously embarrassed. If it weren't for the fact that I've got to go and perform on a stage in a few hours, I would never leave the house again. I can barely bring myself to write it down, but I suppose I have to for the sake of posterity. So here's what happened.

When I went down to the kitchen, I almost changed my mind about confronting Jenny. But then I came in and I heard her say, 'Just look how far you've come in the last few weeks! I'm kind of in awe.' And the idea of her fawning over Rachel when really she was stabbing her in the back made me so mad I just said, 'In awe? Oh, is that what you call it?' in a really snarky voice.

Rachel and Jenny both stared at me.

'Sorry?' said Jenny.

'You heard what I said,' I said.

'Well, yeah,' said Jenny. 'But I don't know what you meant. Seriously, Bex, you've been really weird and off with me lately. Is there anything wrong?'

I snorted in a rather undignified way.

'As if you don't know!' I said.

'I don't!' said Jenny. 'And I'm starting to get tired of it!'

'Well, good,' I said rudely.

'What on earth are you talking about, Bex?' said Rachel. 'And why the hell are you being so obnoxious?'

I swallowed. I knew what I was going to say would break Rachel's heart, and I didn't want to do it, but I knew it had to be done.

'It's Jenny,' I said. 'She's having an affair with Tom.'

I expected Jenny to go white with shock and deny it all, and I assumed Rachel would start wailing or burst into tears or even hit Jenny. But none of these things happened.

In fact, what happened first was that Jenny burst out laughing. And not fake 'Ha-ha-ha' laughing, proper, genuine, wheezy laughing.

'Oh my GOD,' she said. 'Where did that come from?'

And Rachel didn't look upset. She just looked amused and baffled.

'Bex, Jenny is not having an affair with Tom,' she said.

'But I saw them!' I said. 'A few weeks ago! Sitting in the window of a café on Wicklow Street!'

Rachel turned to Jenny. 'Isn't that where you met him to give back his stupid books?' she said.

'Yeah,' said Jenny. 'And she's right, we were near the window.'

She looked at me. 'God, Bex, why on earth did you think I was having an affair with him? Rachel asked me to meet Tom to give back some of his books and stuff. So I did.'

'But …' I said. 'But why did you hang around having a coffee with him? You looked like you were having a really intense conversation!'

'Well, I suppose we were,' said Jenny. 'He was asking me how Rachel was and I was telling him that she was doing amazingly – of course – but that he'd really upset her just dumping her out of the blue. And he felt guilty without feeling sorry for her, which is exactly what we wanted to happen.'

'I knew all about it,' said Rachel. 'We'd spent ages talking about what she'd say to him to make him think I had moved on and wasn't thinking about him at all.'

'But it did look …' I said. 'I mean, Jenny could still have been carrying on with him! She was leaning over and giving him something!' But even as I said it, I realised what she'd been giving him.

'Bex, I'm sorry to burst your bubble, but I'm seeing someone else,' said Jenny. 'His name is Fionn. Seriously, I wouldn't have time to have an affair even if I wanted to, which I don't, and even if I did, I'd never even contemplate having one with Tom. And what I was giving him was Rachel's books.'

'Oh,' I said.

'So do you believe me now?' said Jenny.

'Um, yes,' I said. 'Sorry. About yelling at you. And not believing you.'

'It's okay,' said Jenny.

'And, um, about being weird to you over the last few weeks,' I said. 'I just thought you had stabbed Rachel in the back. And, um, I was just upset about it.'

'Ah, I understand,' said Jenny.

Rachel was looking at me with a funny expression on her face.

'You should have just said something to me,' she said. And I thought she was going to yell at me for not saying anything when I thought her best friend was having a secret affair with her ex. 'But I suppose you were just worried about me.' She paused. 'You're not the worst sister in the world.'

Which, from a member of my family, who are not prone to declarations of love (I found it very difficult when I wrote a song for Rachel's birthday a few months ago), is quite something, especially on top of her thanking me for cheering her up on Tuesday. There was a long pause.

'So ...' I said. 'I suppose I'd better go and get ready for the gig.'

'We'll be there,' said Jenny, who I must admit was

behaving very decently for someone who'd just been accused by me of betraying her best friend and having a secret affair. 'And Fionn is going to meet us there. So you can see I'm not making him up.'

'I don't think you're making him up!' I said miserably. I felt like a giant fool. And then I basically ran up here to my room, where I am writing this while the shame is still fresh.

I am really glad that Jenny isn't having an affair with Tom, though. And at least I don't have to worry about keeping a terrible secret from Rachel anymore. And, actually, I feel a bit less ridiculous having written it all down. It's strange what a relief writing about bad stuff can be. And I do have to get ready for the gig now. I am still feeling quite butterflies-in-the-tummy about it. I still can't help thinking something exciting is going to happen, apart from the whole gig stuff, which is exciting in itself. It just feels like today will be a Big Day.

Right. I've really got to change and get ready at last. I wish I'd asked Rachel if I could borrow some of her posh make-up before I went down and embarrassed myself – I don't feel like creeping in and asking for a favour now. I'll just have to make do with my own non-posh stuff. And I'm going to wear my brilliant '60s brown and gold dress that I got in a charity shop at the end of the summer. Not only does it look cool, it's not too tight so it's particularly easy to drum in. I do like it when clothes are practical as well as cute.

Okay, I really am going now. I won't think about what I said to Jenny at all. I'm going to think about the gig. And about seeing Sam. And what might happen. Because I really do have a feeling that something will.

LATER

Well, first things first. Our gig was brilliant. At least, it went pretty well as far as we were concerned, and the crowd seemed to like it. And there was a pretty big crowd too. But – and I feel kind of stupid even being a bit sad about this when our gig went so well, but after all you can't help how your heart feels – nothing happened with Sam. I mean, I was talking to him a lot. And I was trying to get that balance between being friendly and too friendly. And we did talk on our own for a while. But nothing really happened. By which I mean we didn't start kissing passionately by the speakers (or anywhere else, for that matter), and we didn't declare our undying love (or even mild affection) for each other. So much for my butterflies.

It all happened like this. All four bands only had time to do a quick soundcheck, so we didn't really get a chance to properly see what the other bands were doing. We did get to talk to Veronica and Paul, the sound engineer, about our backdrop, and she promised to get it up just before we went on. Then she told us the running order of the show – first Bad Monkey, then Puce, then us, then the Wicked Ways. And then all four bands just stood around a bit nervously waiting for the main doors to open (well, some of us were nervous. Puce were in a corner practising their stage moves). Some of the others had sneaked cans in, but they were too nervous to take them out and drink anything, mostly because it had been made quite clear that if Veronica saw any booze on the premises, we'd all be kicked out (and, she'd warned us before, there'd be no chance of any more all-ages gigs there).

'What if no one turns up?' said Katie from Bad Monkey. 'I mean, the Battle of the Bands was full, but there were a million bands playing then and everyone brought their friends ...'

But then the door to the venue was pulled back and lots of people started to pour in.

'Whoah,' said Alice, a few minutes later. 'I didn't think it'd be this jammed.'

'Neither did I,' said Richard. 'We'll all be fine though.' He was wearing his specially altered suit and looked very cool. His quiff was at full blast, but he can really pull it off.

'Look, there's Tall Paula and Sophie!' said Cass, giving them a wave. 'And – wow, Small Paula too. I didn't know if she'd come along.'

'And there's Jane and Aoife,' said Alice. Aoife is Jane's best friend. 'Hey, over here!'

I must admit that as soon as the doors opened I started looking out for Sam. Every time a tall boy with scruffy hair walked in my stomach felt all funny because I thought it was him. And then, while I was telling Jane and Aoife about how we'd made our backdrop (Jane is very interested in all things vaguely theatrical), Sam walked in with Lucy and a boy I'd never seen before.

Lucy waved when she saw us and the three of them came over to join us.

'Hey, band people,' said Sam. 'This is Daire.'

'Hey,' said Daire. He was a tall, friendly-looking boy holding a skateboard. 'Ah, hi, Richard.' I forgot they were all in the same school. 'I've heard a lot about all these bands,' Daire went on. 'Sam and Lucy say you're all pretty good ...'

'Well, they might have exaggerated a bit,' said Alice nervously. 'Don't get your hopes up too much.'

'Any nerves, Bex?' said Sam.

'Not really,' I said. 'That's not tempting fate, is it? Maybe it would be better if I was really nervous ...'

'Nah,' said Sam. 'I don't believe in tempting fate anyway. You'll all be brilliant.'

I wish he hadn't said that 'all'. I wish he'd singled us out. Anyway, then Alice said, 'Hey, Emma's arrived. And look who's with her!'

It was Alison! And Karen was nowhere to be seen. Alison has clearly escaped from her clutches at last. She looked a bit shy when she and Emma joined us, but soon she and Emma were talking to Daire, whose brother, it turns out, goes to the same computer course as them.

'Wow, Dublin really is small,' I said.

'Well, our bit of north Dublin definitely is,' said Sam.

And then I noticed Rachel come in with Jenny and another boy I'd never seen before. I realised it must be Fionn, Jenny's actual boyfriend. He must definitely really like her if he's willing to come and see her best friend's little sister's band. I still felt too embarrassed to talk to them, but I couldn't avoid doing so because Jenny yelled 'Rebecca! Over here!' in a loud voice, so I had to trot over to them.

'Look what a good sister I am,' said Rachel. 'Bringing along some more people to cheer for you so it's not too embarrassing later.'

'Hey, Bex,' said Jenny, grinning at me. 'This is Fionn. Fionn, as you've gathered, this is Rebecca.'

'Hi,' said Fionn. He was a cheerful-looking boy with fair hair and a nice cardigan. And he didn't look anything at all like Tom.

'I've told him all about you,' said Jenny.

I knew she was enjoying my embarrassment, but I suppose it was what I deserved. Anyway, I didn't stay talking to them for long because the main lights in the venue were getting dimmer, which meant the show was about to begin. Bad Monkey were on first and I was really looking forward to seeing them because the only time I've ever seen them perform was a year ago at the Battle of the Bands.

'Good luck!' said Rachel.

'You'll be great,' said Jenny, winking at me, and I knew things would be okay between us. She clearly has a forgiving nature. I think I'd have let someone suffer for a bit longer if they'd accused me of being a friend-betrayer.

'Hi, everyone!' said Veronica. 'I'm very happy to welcome you all to what will hopefully be the first of many all-ages gigs here at the Knitting Factory. We've got four brilliant bands playing this afternoon, so without further ado please give a warm welcome to ... Bad Monkey!'

I was very impressed with Bad Monkey back at the Battle of the Bands, even though they only did two songs, and this time they were even better. Liz is such a cool frontwoman, I couldn't take my eyes off her. I don't fancy girls, but I can definitely see why Cass likes her so much. The crowd were clearly impressed too, judging by the wild cheers when she played her guitar solo (she'd been worried that she was going to mess it up, but it sounded perfect).

When they came off stage Liz ran over to Cass, who gave her a big hug, and we all congratulated her.

'I can't believe we made it through a whole set!' she said. 'We haven't played in front of an audience for so long!'

'It doesn't show,' said Cass. 'You were amazing!'

'You were fantastic!' said Lucy, who had never seen Bad Monkey play before. 'I didn't realise you could play such fancy stuff on the guitar.'

'Ooh, what's going on now?' said Ellie, pointing at the stage.

It was Puce, arranging their stage set. Or rather, helping Veronica pull down a screen at the back of the stage. A few moments later, they had taken their positions and Veronica was announcing them to the crowd. We all cheered loudly as

Niall took to the mike.

'We're Puce!' he cried. 'And we're going to take you to another world! A world ... of robots!'

Then, as the band started playing, the screen behind them was filled with old black and white footage of robots. And, as if that wasn't enough, Niall and the others started doing some dramatic moves – not just prowling around the stage as Shane from The Invited had taught them, but some coordinated dance moves that mimicked the motion of the robots. It was all very impressive. The music was, as ever, a little bit dull, but to be honest what with the dancing and the robots you barely noticed.

In fact, I don't think I was giving Puce the attention they deserved because I was standing next to Sam and I was kind of conscious of him all the time. Also, I was getting nervous about going on next. But anyway, by the time Puce finished the audience were all cheering like mad.

Sam leaned over to me.

'Did you ever think of having projections and stuff?' he said over the wild applause. 'That looked really good!'

'Don't let Cass hear you say that,' I said. 'It'll only encourage her. Right, we're on next. I'd better go.'

'Good luck!' said Sam. 'I'll be dancing in the front row.'

I knew he was joking, but it would have been very cool if he had been. And when we got on stage I could see he was up near the front with all our friends (and Rachel, Jenny and Fionn too). Just behind them I could see our mentor Kitty, who caught my eye and gave me a thumbs up. While we were setting up our instruments, Veronica and Paul hung up the backdrop. It looked really good. You'd never guess it had been one of Cass's parents' old bed sheets until a week ago.

'Right,' said Cass, as we took our positions. 'Our biggest gig ever. No pressure!'

'We thrive under pressure,' said Alice grandly, and picked up the microphone. She has real stage presence. No wonder she and Richard make such a good couple.

'Hey, we're Hey Dollface,' she said. 'And we're going to start with a song about falling for the wrong person. One, two, three, four!'

We launched into 'Ever Saw In You', with lyrics all about me and John Kowalski. As I drummed along furiously, I found myself wondering if Sam would realise what it was about, and would he know that I wasn't, like, harbouring any feelings for John. But soon I got so into playing I forgot to think about Sam, or anything else but how cool it felt to be up on the stage playing music with my best friends. When we finished the first song, the crowd all cheered and hollered very loudly, and Cass and Alice and I beamed at each other before Cass announced the next song, 'Pistachio'. After every song, I found myself counting how many songs we had left, not because I wanted it to end but because I wanted it to last as long as possible. We made a few tiny mistakes, but I don't think anyone really noticed, and when we finished the last song (our environmental anthem 'Living in a Bubble') everyone cheered and cheered. It felt brilliant.

When we got back to our friends, everyone was very enthusiastic. Kitty ran over and hugged us all and told us she was proud of us, which was lovely.

'I can't wait to see what you do next!' she said.

Small Paula, who is of course a girl of few words, just nodded at us and said, 'Very nice work.' Which is high praise from her.

And Sam was enthusiastic too.

'That was amazing!' he said. 'You were all even better than when you played at the camp.'

I was on such a high I forgot to be self-conscious.

'Really? Thanks!' I said. 'It was so much fun.'

'How do you play the drums with your feet and hands at the same time?' said Sam. 'I've always wondered about that.

I'm pretty sure I'd get something confused.'

'Ah, it's not that hard,' I said, and it isn't now, even though when I first got my drum kit I was horrified to discover that I had to use a pedal as well as the drumsticks to play some of the drums and I got totally confused myself. 'Hey, look, the Wicked Ways are on now.'

Richard and his friends were on stage and ready to go. A spotlight shone on one of the mikes, and Richard walked up to it.

'Wow, his suit looks so cool!' said Cass. 'I think it might be even better than his brother's one. I mean, it's basically made to measure.'

'Welcome, welcome,' said Richard in the booming voice he adopts on stage, a voice that should be ridiculous but is somehow impressive. 'We're the Wicked Ways. I'm Richard Murray. And I'm a fool for love.'

They launched into their song 'Fool For Love', which involves him doing even more booming than usual. The first time I saw them perform it, I thought it was ridiculous, but it quickly grew on me.

The audience liked it too. In fact, by the time the band did their song 'Pterodactyl' and Richard was singing about 'Flying over unforgiving lands / Wishing that I had human hands ...'

he had the crowd eating out of his (human) hands. It was really good. Alice looked very proud. I wonder what their musical collaboration will sound like? She does a lot less bellowing than him (though she too is a very confident performer). Anyway, when they finished they got a huge cheer, and then Veronica came out and thanked everyone for coming.

'And the biggest thanks of all go to our four bands, Bad Monkey, Puce, Hey Dollface and of course Richard Murray and the Wicked Ways. Give them a big round of applause!'

The crowd went wild, and then it was over. Except it wasn't over, for us. Rachel, Jenny and Fionn went off (Jenny even gave me a hug. She really is quite noble) and then all four bands and some of our friends like Jane and Ellie and of course Sam, Lucy and Senan all went back to the art space, where Veronica had laid out some snacks and soft drinks as a special reward for us being the stars of the first all-ages band afternoon.

'You've got this space for an hour and a half,' she said. 'And I'll be checking in on you. So don't mess it up.'

It was like a party. Well, basically it was a party. It was dark outside and the only lighting came from the lamps over the drawing boards, which helped create a party-ish mood. Liz had brought little speakers and plugged in her phone so we had some music. Someone produced some of the cans, the contents of which were discreetly poured into mugs from the art space kitchen. But I didn't have more than a sip because I don't really like beer, and I was also totally paranoid about Veronica finding out and banning us all from the Knitting Factory forever. In fact, I was glad when the beer ran out (quite quickly as it happened, because they didn't have many cans and there were loads of us).

I was talking to lots of people, but, like the last time we all hung out in the art space, I was always conscious of Sam, of where he was and who he was talking to, and of the fact that we weren't talking to each other and that time was going by very quickly. And then, when I went over to the table to refill my glass (just Coke, I might add), he came over.

'Hello, drumming sensation,' he said. 'Having fun?'

'I'm still in a bit of a daze,' I said.

'Well, you were great,' he said, smiling. He has a very nice smile. 'I look forward to the next one. Next gig, I mean.'

And then there was a pause, and maybe it was because I'd spent so much time convincing myself that something was going to happen today, but suddenly everything felt sort of intense and strange. Like, well, like something might happen.

Then he asked me if we'd thought any more about recording stuff, and I told him maybe at Christmas, and he said he'd do some artwork for us if we liked, but I was barely listening to what he was saying because I was so conscious of the two of us, together, and somehow we ended up on the side of the room where fewer people were and he said something about feeling really at home in the studio, and I was sure, absolutely sure, that something would happen, because everything seemed so, I dunno, intimate. We got talking about the future and about Sam's comics and how he was going to enter the one he showed me last week in a big competition.

'I know the chances of winning anything are small,' he said. 'But I want to give it a try.'

'You should definitely go for it,' I said.

'Well, if I win, I'll thank you in my acceptance speech,' he said. 'You can do the same for me whenever you win a, well, whatever the big awards for cool indie bands are.'

'It's a deal,' I said. And we kept talking about nonsense, and it was fun. But as it got later and later my hope that SOMETHING was going to happen between us gradually trickled away. I knew we were all going to have to go home eventually, and the time was getting closer and closer. But even though we'd talked on our own and it had felt so weird and intense for a while, he hadn't made any sort of move. And I hadn't done anything either. And just as I was thinking about this Veronica came in and said, 'Right, ladies and gentlemen, time to go!'

I was wondering if we'd go on somewhere else, though I'm not sure where I thought we could go at half six on a Saturday. It's not like we could go to a pub. Also, I needed to get home for dinner. Then Lucy said she'd better go home, and then someone else said they needed to as well, so that was that. We all headed outside.

'If I spend any longer at the Knitting Factory on Saturdays, my parents are going to stop me going at all,' said Niall. 'Exams, and all that.'

'Is anyone free tomorrow?' said Tall Paula. 'Why don't we have one last afternoon meet-up before we have to really knuckle down?'

'I have to go to my aunt's house,' said Sophie regretfully.

'I should be able to wangle it,' said Cass. 'What about you, Bex?'

'Oh yeah, probably,' I said.

'I'll try and make it,' said Sam. 'But I'll have to check with my folks. I think there's something on tomorrow.'

Most of the others said they could make it too, so we're going to meet tomorrow. I hope Sam comes, though knowing my luck he won't. And even if he did, if nothing is going to happen when we're all at a party (well, sort of party), then I doubt anything will happen in the Flapper Café in the middle of the afternoon.

So yeah. I walked to the bus stop with Cass and Lucy, and Daire and Sam went off to their bus stop, and that was that. I feel kind of silly about having got my hopes up. I mean, really there was no reason to assume something was going to happen. Or, I suppose, that something will ever happen. And I also just feel sad about it. Because I really like him, and I want to be with him, and even though being friends with him is great, it's not quite enough for me.

I suppose I'll just have to wait until it wears off. Which I know it will. Eventually. Everything does, as I found out with Paperboy (and as Rachel is sort of finding out about Tom). I'll just hope that he doesn't start going out with someone else before then. I don't think I could bear that. I don't think I could be friends with him anymore if that happened.

But, at the same time, I'm not totally miserable, because when I think about us playing up on that stage, I just feel really happy. It's such a brilliant feeling to do something you love and do it well. It's especially good when other people like it, of course, but even when we're just practising, I love it when a song comes together. It's not like any other feeling in the world. And it's even better when you feel it in front of your friends (and your sister and the person you unfairly accused of being a traitor a few hours ago). So apart from that very embarrassing moment this morning, it should have been a very cool day. And it was.

But at the same time I feel so disappointed about Sam, and then I feel stupid for being disappointed. It's very weird. I wonder if feeling loads of things at the same time is normal? I suppose it must be. I mean, so much of life is a sort of mixture. Anyway, I'm not going to get my hopes up about tomorrow. I'll just feel miserable if nothing happens AGAIN. He probably won't even turn up.

I'm relieved I'm allowed to go out at all, though. When I mentioned it to Mum and Dad this evening, they started grumbling about how I was never home, but then I reminded them that they'd said 'Back to work on Monday!' and I promised to do all my homework before I went out tomorrow so they grudgingly agreed.

I don't know what to wear tomorrow. I was thinking of wearing the dress that I wore for our first Knitting Factory gig. It might be a lucky dress because I was wearing it when Paperboy first kissed me, but then it was also what I was wearing when I fell backwards off the drum platform. Hmmm.

Maybe I should wear my dress with the stripy navy and

white top bit and a flared navy skirt bit. It makes me look like I have slightly more bosom than I actually do (not that that's saying very much) AND it's really comfy so it's perfect. And Sam has never seen it before so maybe he'll be dazzled by it. But like I said, I don't want to get my hopes up. I really don't want to be disappointed again.

SUNDAY ☼

Wow. Today did not go exactly as I thought it would. To say the least. I'm still in a bit of a daze, to be honest. But a good sort of daze. Definitely a good sort of daze.

It started out very boringly. As promised, I did my home-work nice and early and even showed it to my parents so they could see I was working nice and hard.

'Look!' I said dramatically, waving an English essay at them. 'Now do you believe that I'm on top of my schoolwork?'

'We do trust you, Bex,' said Dad. 'We just want to make sure you take your studying seriously this year. Learning how to knuckle down to hard work is very important.'

I could have said something about people who seem to spend more time on their Henry Higgins dances than their actual job, but I didn't want to push my luck. So I borrowed a fiver off him and went in to meet the others.

I was running a bit late and when I got to the Flapper Café Cass, Liz, Richard, Alice, Lucy, Tall Paula and Sophie were there already. But no Sam. I didn't even feel surprised. I'd had a feeling he wouldn't come. Obviously, it was cool to see all the others, but I was still really disappointed. I tried not to show it, of course.

'No Sam today?' I asked Lucy, but only after we'd been talking for a few minutes. I didn't want it to be the first thing out of my mouth.

'No, he had to go and visit his new baby cousin this morning,' said Lucy.

I might have known. Stupid babies! Still ruining my social life. I hoped this one hadn't headbutted him. Babies can be very violent.

Anyway, I tried not to think about him and just enjoy the afternoon. And it really was fun. Cass was planning to go back to Liz's house afterwards for their first musical collaboration attempt.

'I'll have to use Liz's sister's old keyboard,' she said. 'But it'll do for now.'

Alice was going to Richard's for dinner, but she said they

wouldn't have time to do any music stuff because her dad was coming to pick her up at half seven.

'As soon as I'm old enough to legally drive, I'm going to beg my parents for lessons,' she said. 'Living out in the wilds wouldn't be half as bad if I didn't have to rely on them for lifts all the time.'

'Small Paula can drive,' said Tall Paula. We all stared at her. 'Seriously! I know it's illegal, but she can. She told me her aunt taught her. She can drive a tractor too.'

'Is there anything Small Paula can't do?' said Richard admiringly.

It was almost starting to get dark when we all left and said our goodbyes. I was walking down the road with Liz and Cass when I realised I'd forgotten something.

'My scarf!' I said. 'It must be on my chair. I'd better go back.'

'We'll wait here for you,' said Cass.

'Ah, don't bother,' I said. 'We're not going the same way, anyway. Go and write some amazing electro-pop songs!'

'We'll do our best,' said Liz.

'See you on Monday!' said Cass.

I went back to the café, feeling a bit sorry for myself. Everyone seemed to be all happily coupled up apart from me. Well, me and Lucy. And Paula and Sophie. But still.

My scarf was hanging on the back of the chair where I'd left it, so I grabbed it and headed back out. It was chilly and I felt even more sorry for myself as I turned in the direction of the bus stop. And then I saw something that made me freeze in my tracks. Running up the road towards me, his portfolio bag hanging from one shoulder, was Sam.

'Oh good, you're still here!' he said breathlessly, coming to a halt outside the café. 'I thought I'd missed you all. The bus broke down and was stuck at the side of the road for ages. And my stupid phone died so I couldn't text any of you.'

'Well, I'm the only one left,' I said. 'The others have gone. Were you looking for Lucy?'

'No, actually it was you I wanted to see,' said Sam. He leaned over and took a deep breath. 'God, I need to get fitter. I just ran from the bus stop, but I feel like I'm dying.'

'What ...' I said. The butterflies started fluttering in my tummy again. 'What did you want to see me for?'

'Ah,' said Sam. He looked a bit flustered, but I thought he could just still be out of breath. 'I just wanted to talk to you and ... I wanted to give you this.'

He took a piece of paper out of his portfolio bag and handed it to me. It was a picture of me, drawn in the style of his comics. There was nothing cutesy about it. It was funny and cool and it really did look like me but with slightly better hair. I was leaning on a pile of books with my drum sticks in one hand and a pen in the other, and I was wearing what looked like my brown '60s dress. It was the best picture I've ever seen in my life.

'Sam!' I said. 'That's amazing! But ...'

'And there's something else,' said Sam. 'Something I want to say and I've got to say it now or I'll never say it at all.' He took a deep breath. 'I have no idea whether you feel the same way, but I know I just need to tell you how much I like you. And NOT just as a friend. And if you don't feel the same way, that's cool, I wasn't just hanging out with you because I thought I'd get anything out of it, but I just needed to tell you that I really liked you because if there was a chance you liked me back, I needed to ...'

But before he finished the sentence, I leaned over and kissed him. I didn't even think about it. I just did it.

And straight away he was kissing me back, and there was something about it, something different to kissing Paperboy or John Kowalski. It was better. With Paperboy I was madly in love with him, but I never really knew him – I mean, when he first kissed me, we'd only talked for about ten minutes altogether. And with John, I really, really fancied him, but I don't think I actually liked him very much.

But with Sam ... I really fancy him, but I also like him. I know him. We're actual friends. And I've wanted this to happen for ages and ages, and then finally it did, and a part of me felt it was almost too good to be true, but mostly it just felt ... right. It was the best of everything, all coming together at once. It was brilliant.

We stood there kissing for ages, and finally we drew apart and stared at each other.

'Wow,' said Sam, and smiled. 'So ... you don't feel the same way, then?'

And I laughed, and he laughed, and then I kissed him again, and he kissed me back, and I felt very, very happy. And when we eventually stopped, he took my hand and we walked down the street in a sort of happy daze.

'I've liked you for ages too,' I said. 'I think I liked you in the summer.'

'Well, I noticed you when I first saw you at the musical,' said Sam. 'But then you were with John, so I sort of stopped thinking of you in that way. And then, in the summer, after we'd got friendly at the camp, I suppose I started, well, thinking of you like that again.'

'I'm glad you did,' I said.

He squeezed my hand tightly.

'Me too,' he said.

And we walked down to my bus stop together, and he's going to message me later, and we're hopefully going to meet after school during the week (just for a few minutes. I'm not going to push it with my parents), and of course we'll see each other properly next Saturday.

And I feel so happy about all of it. I don't think I've ever known a boy who seems to get me like Sam gets me. I really like him and I fancy him and we just ... get on with each other. He's funny and nice and smart and he loves making stuff and reading stuff and he gets on with my friends and ... it already works. We work. I really think we'll be very good together. I mean, I suppose I could be wrong about this.

But I'm pretty sure I'm right.

THE END

The END

THE REAL REBECCA

My name is Rebecca Rafferty, and my mother has ruined my life. Again. I didn't mind her writing boring books for grown-ups. But now she's written one about an awful girl my age and everyone thinks it's me! Including the boy who delivers our newspapers, aka Paperboy, aka the most gorgeous boy in the whole world. Oh, the shame!

And if that wasn't awful enough, the biggest pain in my class wants to use my 'fame' to get herself on the reality show *My Big Birthday Bash*.

I've just got to show everyone the REAL Rebecca. But how?

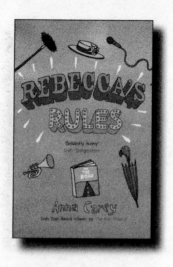

REBECCA RULES

1. My boyfriend has moved to Canada. Canada!
2. I have annoyed my best friends Cass and Alice by going on about him all the time.
3. I am going to a crazy girl's mad birthday party and I am not sure why.

Things have got to change. So I've made some new rules.

No moping.

No ignoring my friends' problems.

Find something exciting for me, Cass and Alice to do so our friendship gets back to normal.

Something fun. Something new ....

Something like joining the school musical.

REBECCA ROCKS

My name is Rebecca Rafferty, and I know that this is
going to be the BEST summer ever.

Well, maybe.

Holidays mean no school for three months! And
my band Hey Dollface are going to a cool summer
camp to (hopefully) become total rock stars.

But there's another band – the Crack Parrots,
a gang of 'mean boys' – and they're going to be trouble.

And as for romance, my friend Cass's love life is
complicated and my own love life doesn't really exist at
all ...